# ROAD TO RICHES

## The Great Railroad Race to Aspen

By Cathy L. Clamp and C. T. Adams

WESTERN REFLECTIONS
PUBLISHING COMPANY®

Montrose, Colorado

© 2003 Cathy L. Clamp and C. T. Adams

ISBN 1-890437-84-0

Library of Congress Control Number: 2003102303

First Edition
Printed in the United States of America

Cover photo: D&RG Construction Train heading toward Glenwood Springs. (W. H. Jackson photo: Denver Public Library Western History Department, #WHJ-1637)

Cover and text design by Laurie Goralka Design

Western Reflections Publishing Company®
219 Main Street
Montrose, CO 81401
www.westernreflectionspub.com

# DEDICATION

The authors would like to dedicate this book to their families and friends. Most particularly, Cathy's wonderful husband, Don, for both his technical assistance (is there *anything* that man doesn't know?!) and his loving support and encouragement, and to C's fabulous son, James, for his patience and unwavering confidence. We would like to take this opportunity to thank everyone who believed in us and, individually and collectively, offered their support over the years. We also (but not equally) dedicate this work to the people who *didn't* believe in us — who said it was a pipe dream and couldn't be done. The desire to prove you wrong gave us the stubbornness to see this through when things got tough. Sometimes it's good to be contrary.

# ACKNOWLEDGMENTS

There are many people and organizations who deserve acknowledgment for this book. Thanks go, first of all, to those who read and made suggestions on the book itself. To Art Pansing, who read the short story, and said, "Write a novel!" Suzanne Burris, the Curator/Archivist of The Burlington Northern and Santa Fe Railway Company, was especially helpful in finding civil engineering documents of the time. Connie Menninger, Curator of the Santa Fe Railway Project for the Kansas State Historical Society sent pages and pages of background material. Ken Forrest, Chuck Albi, and the staff of the Colorado Railroad Museum Collection in Golden were cooperative and helpful, as were the staff of the Denver Public Library Western History Department and Colorado Historical Society Stephen H. Hart Library. Thanks to you all for your work on our behalf in putting together the chronology of this wonderful story. We would also like to express our sympathy to the family of Jackson C. Thode, LM, a great railroad historian who recently passed on. We wished we could have met you.

# AUTHOR'S NOTES

This is a work of fiction, but the events that occurred are real.

The battle between the Denver and Rio Grande Railroad and the Colorado Midland Railroad was well known in railroad circles, but very little of the race to Aspen was known to the general public.

What emerged from a simple, cursory research project to do a short story were snippets of a riveting tale. But only snippets. Few records were kept from that time. The more information we gathered, the more complex the story became. From political backstabbing to multiple levels of saboteurs, the real story was an eloquent tale of hard-working, proud men, building a route to the silver fields of Aspen, against the odds of weather and geography, and various factions trying to prevent their success. The truth was as good a story as a writer could hope for, so all we did was embellish a bit.

It was 1887. Colorado had been a state for just eleven years. Most of the Western Slope of Colorado received freight by stage and wagon traffic, a long and arduous trip over the Continental Divide. The Denver & Rio Grande (D&RG), known as the "Baby Road," had just been reorganized by bankruptcy courts. The investors of the new company resided in London. They were skittish about wasting money and didn't understand the politics of the little backwater of Colorado. Because of the bankruptcy, other railroads weren't taking the Baby Road seriously. The Atchison, Topeka & Santa Fe broke "The Treaty of Boston" which forbade the Kansas Road from building in D&RG territory. The Union Pacific was buying up smaller companies to cut into the D&RG's business. The officers of the D&RG, who lived in Colorado, realized that whoever reached Aspen first could write their own ticket on passengers seeking new vacation spots, and on freight of both silver ore and coal. William Jackson and David Moffatt closed their eyes, crossed their fingers, and dove into the battle with fists and money flying.

The Colorado Midland had a head start. Jackson knew from his own spies when the Midland expected to reach Aspen. The Union Pacific, the D&RG's chief rival, was busy charting their own course to Aspen from Grand Junction. This information panicked Jackson and Moffatt. They convinced the board of directors in New York to fund the construction without the approval of the investors. In March of 1887, they started building from Red Cliff, near Vail, using 1,000 men and over 600 animals. The construction crew traveled eighty-six miles from Red Cliff to Aspen–in eight months! They paid the men nearly double the standard wage in order to keep enough men working. The first train rolled into Aspen on November 1, 1887. They constructed a combination standard and narrow gauge bed, a technique which slowed down construction immensely. However, making the ties wide enough to later lay a third rail ensured the D&RG of a future, because standard gauge was becoming the norm. In addition, a fully loaded locomotive could only scale a maximum of a two percent grade, so they had to flatten miles and miles of mountain terrain.

Most of the characters are completely real. If we could find the names of real people doing real jobs, we used them. However, many are fictional or a combination of people. Most of the construction workers and other day-to-day employees of the D&RG are anonymous, except for their initials on a document. Where we could find last names, we found no first name. If we got the given name, the surname was lacking. So we created names and personalities. We tried to make real people out of paper names. However, if we have characterized an ancestor of yours, and got the name or personality wrong, be gentle. We tried — really.

# PROLOGUE

"GEE-UP!" boomed a voice through the blinding rain. The sharp crack of a whip followed the words, and twin Belgian horses strained against their harnesses to obey. Gale force winds pushed against the horses' powerful muscles, but they slowly made headway through the storm. A mud-encrusted length of steel crawled out of the surging river and came to rest on the sand beside a stack of similar rails.

A tall figure in an oilskin duster strode angrily up to the scene. The driver of the horses looked anxious as he approached.

"That's the last of them, Boss," he said placatingly.

"Whose dang-fool idea was that stunt?" the newcomer called through a wet kerchief over his face.

The driver kept his head tipped down to prevent his hat from blowing away. "The river weren't so high a few minutes ago, Luke," he shouted over the howling wind. Even to him it sounded a weak excuse.

Luke Ballister, gang boss of the Colorado Springs to Pueblo spur, removed his kerchief, exposing his face to the stinging rain, and glared at the driver with flashing green eyes. "I asked you whose idea it was!"

"See," began the man nervously, not meeting the eyes of the taller man while he unchained the steel rail from the hitching chain, "Ben and me thought that it would be a lot quicker to move the rails to the new site if we floated them on the river."

Luke looked at him incredulously, and had to shut his mouth against the rain. "You thought five tons of steel rail would *float*?"

"Well," replied the driver slowly, "with a big enough raft . . . ."

Luke shook his head as he tried to grasp the concept. "Tom, a raft big enough to float that much steel on a river this little is called a *bridge*!"

Tom winced at the obvious sarcasm.

Luke had opened his mouth to continue the reprimand when the sound of pounding hooves and furious splashes caught his attention. He turned to see a lone rider, head bowed low over his horse's neck, galloping toward them.

He dismissed Tom with an angry wave of his hand. "Get that steel loaded back on the flatbed and rub down those horses! They've done their share for today."

Luke walked toward where the rider was dismounting. He could read the yellow lettering of the Western Union on the oiled saddlebags.

"Can I help you?" Luke asked.

"Looking for a Colonel Ballister," the rider shouted. "I have an urgent telegram."

Luke started at the name. Colonel — now, there was a title Luke hadn't heard in a while. He'd stopped using his war title when the war ended. Many men would use the title they'd earned forever. Luke had done so himself for a time. It was just that the war had been so hard, so bloody, and so damn *long* ago. He wanted to forget. Get on with his life. He was *Mister* Ballister now.

"I'm Colonel Ballister," Luke replied cautiously. Who could possibly be trying to reach him using that name?

"You'll have to sign for it," the rider said. "Can we get out of this storm?"

Luke couldn't think of anything he would enjoy more. He led the driver to the rail car that served as an office. "Atchison, Topeka & Santa Fe" was painted in tall, bright letters on the side of the car. Once inside, Luke gratefully removed his soaked hat. The Western Union driver did the same. He then pulled an oilskin sleeve from beneath his poncho and handed Luke the cable.

Luke had no way to dry his hands. Everything in the car was rain-soaked from repeated door openings, so he simply did his best not to smear the ink on the paper. He signed for the cable on the line of the log where the messenger indicated. The man then carefully replaced the log under his poncho. He put on his hat and pulled it down tight, opened the door to the car, and bulled his way back into the storm to make his next delivery.

Luke carefully opened the outer covering and unfolded the thick yellow paper. The cable was brief.

GREETINGS COLONEL — STOP — HAVE URGENT NEED OF YOUR SERVICES — STOP — DRG OFFERING $200 TO MEET WITH YOU — STOP — PERSONAL FAVOR TO ME — STOP — LEAVE IMMEDIATELY TO MEET WITH JACKSON DRG OFFICES LARIMER STREET — STOP — $100 ALREADY WAITING IN YOUR NAME AT WELLS FARGO LITTLE LONDON — STOP — OTHER $100 WHEN YOU ARRIVE — STOP — WITH FOND REGARDS GENERAL PALMER

The name made Luke smile, and he spoke to the empty room, "As I live and breathe, General William Jackson Palmer!" He read the telegram through a second time, slowly. Two hundred dollars! What could be important enough to pay him two hundred dollars just to ride to Denver for a meeting? What was important enough for Palmer to pay Western Union to track him down to deliver the telegram?

Luke's head spun with questions. He poured himself a cup of piquant chicory and stared out into the abating storm as he thought about it. A shaft of sunlight broke through the clouds briefly, only to be chased away.

Just a month remained until the job with the AT&SF was completed. He would earn the standard $75 for his work as gang boss. He could nearly triple that money in a single day! Once more, he read the cable. It was the Denver & Rio Grande that wanted his services, not the general. Why was Palmer even helping the D&RG after they'd forced him out? Luke was suspicious by nature. It was how he had survived through the war. The only way he could think of to verify the contents of the cable was to travel to Wells Fargo in Colorado Springs, christened "Little London" by the general himself when he'd founded the town years before.

When work ended for the day, he saddled his horse, Star, and rode the ten miles to Colorado Springs. Sure enough, there was $100 held in his name at the desk, wrapped in official Denver & Rio Grande stationery. He stood in the brightly lit lobby of the Wells Fargo office and made his decision.

# CHAPTER 1

Quiet rain pattered on the long glass window in the darkened hallway. Luke's duster dripped muddy water onto the elegant carpet underfoot. A chill in the air — even inside the Larimer Street office building, told him the rain outside could turn to snow. April weather was unpredictable in Denver. He hoped that one of the infamous spring blizzards wouldn't be the result. He could hear the splashes of shod horses and wagons on the cobbled street below, and a trolley bell rang brightly, oblivious to the weather.

He hesitated before opening the wooden door leading to the office of the Denver & Rio Grande Railway.

"Railroad," he corrected himself sharply, and a little sadly. It's a different company now. This isn't Palmer's "Baby Road" anymore. No, they took it away from the General.

Luke took a deep breath, squared his shoulders, and opened the door. He was surprised to see that the interior of the office still looked the same. White painted walls with dark wood trim. A single desk graced the front room. A rug had been added to the polished wood floors. Luke dripped brownish rain on it as well.

A young clerk sitting at the desk looked up from a thick, red ledger. Luke could see the clerk's fine, spindly handwriting on the ruled paper. Luke removed his hat, and ran fingers through his dark blonde hair, hoping to make it a bit more presentable. A glance at his reflection in the looking glass above the desk showed that it hadn't worked. He put the hat back on.

Unfortunately, he couldn't hide the beard stubble as easily. Luke would have preferred to put on clean clothes and shave before the meeting, but he had been asked to come directly to the office upon arrival. He wished he knew why.

"May I help you?" asked the clerk in a soft tenor, his voice slightly haughty. He seemed just out of primary school. Luke tried to remember when he was as young as the clerk. The boy was scrawny, and had dark hair slicked back in the popular style. His weak chin made his nose look too big. He wore a starched shirt with a collar stiff enough to stand in the corner on its own, and thin, dark suspenders that stood out in sharp relief against the snowy whiteness of his shirt. A small pair of spectacles perched on his nose like some odd insect. He looked a little bored, and not terribly bright. The clerk examined Luke over the top of his spectacles with an expression of disdain.

Luke took mild exception to the look.

He couldn't decide why he felt so edgy, standing here. He had probably been in this office twenty times, and had always felt at home. He shook off the tension visibly and replied to the question with searing politeness. "My name is Luke Ballister. I'm here to see Mr. Jackson."

At this, the clerk's eyes went wide, and his whole attitude changed. Suddenly he was impressed. "Oh! Of course. I'll inform Mr. Jackson you're here, Colonel Ballister."

The clerk moved his chair back without a sound. Luke wondered how. The boy walked quickly to a door that Luke remembered well, knocked, and entered when requested.

Luke took off his brown, split-crown hat, and turned it round and round in his hands. Each nick and cut in the thick felt was evident as the damp brim slid through his fingers. It was a nervous habit. Why did he still feel nervous?

The office was essentially the same, but had a different *feel*, somehow. As though part of its spirit was missing. Before, when General Palmer ran the road, the whole place sort of vibrated with the General's energy, his excitement.

Luke waited for the clerk to return and looked around the room. The furnishings were spare, as always. Two roomy wooden chairs for guests, a table, a coat rack, and the front desk. The rug was new. Something else was different, too. But what?

Ah, that's it!, he thought suddenly. The portrait was missing — between the two long windows on the west wall.

The portrait of General Palmer had always amused Luke. Oh, it was a fine painting, and a good likeness, but Luke couldn't quite understand the ego it would take to have a picture of *yourself* hanging where you spent most of your time.

It made Luke smile suddenly. Ego personified. That was General Palmer. He wasn't a big man, but he had a *presence* that took you by surprise. He was clean shaven when Luke first met him, but Luke remembered that he had a thick, bristly mustache in the portrait. It seemed a lifetime ago that he had met the General on the flats of Pennsylvania.

The inner office door opened, interrupting Luke's musings.

# CHAPTER 2

"Colonel Ballister?" the clerk said politely, and slightly nervously, as he held open the inner door. "They're ready for you."

They?

Luke removed his soggy duster and hung it on the coat rack, and placed his hat on the second wooden knob. It occurred to him that until that moment he believed he would be turned away, money or not.

He made another half-hearted attempt to subdue his hair, then gave up. He walked into the room, past the clerk, and faced two men.

"Thank you, Joshua," said one of the men in a dismissive manner. The clerk quietly shut the door behind him as he left.

He didn't recognize either man. The first sat behind the carved oak desk that had been designed and specially ordered by General Palmer. He was tall, with broad shoulders that filled his jacket fully. A wild, white beard and mustache hid half his face. His bald head was surrounded with a ring of tidy white hair. He looked ill. Not sick like a spring fever, but deeper, more long-term. He had a strong face, and clear, piercing eyes. Whatever the sickness was, it hadn't dulled his mind. His suit was dark and expensive looking, but his hands had worked before. They were rough and calloused.

The other man, seated in a chair to the right of the first man, was shorter and stockier. He had the beginnings of a double chin, and a walrus mustache. His suit was also expensively cut, probably custom made to the man's large frame. Luke guessed that the gentleman had probably never worked a full day outdoors in his life.

The first man stood and offered his hand. "Colonel Ballister," he said, "My name is William Jackson."

Luke shook his hand. Jackson had a firm, strong grip that tested Luke's to the point of effort. Luke had never before met the new president of the D&RG. He only knew that Jackson was formerly the court-appointed receiver for the bankrupt Baby Road.

There was something about Jackson that Luke liked. There was a kinship that told Luke they were both railroad men. "A pleasure, sir," Luke replied cordially.

William Jackson took stock of the man who had come at their call. He had been briefed by Palmer, but William liked to measure a man for himself. Luke Ballister was tall and husky. He had broad shoulders and narrow hips and an unruly shock of golden hair. He had a firm, strong grip, and looked a man in the eye squarely. William approved.

William found it hard to believe that this man had been a full colonel in the Union forces at only sixteen years of age. But Palmer had assured him it was no accident. Luke had earned his rank. Jackson looked him over, taking note of every detail. Ballister wore his holster low on his hip, gunslinger fashion. His polite manner belied a quickness, a certainty of purpose that Jackson wouldn't care to stand against. William could see the intelligence that burned behind intense green eyes. Ballister appeared calm, and slightly curious, not nervous or skittish. But could he truly lead over a thousand men through the wilderness to their goal?

Luke turned to the second man. He sat far enough in the corner to give the impression of distance. Not just physical space, but personal as well. He did not stand. Nor did he offer his hand. His arms remained comfortably on the rests of the chair. His fingers were clasped together over his buttoned vest. He looked Luke over as though inspecting a horse he had purchased.

"I'm David Moffat," he said. A small amount of annoyance played through his voice. "I will be succeeding Mr. Jackson as President of the D&RG at the next stockholder meeting. Mr. Jackson felt it was important for both of us to meet with you. I don't agree, but I'm here in any event."

Luke raised his eyebrows. He hadn't realized there was to be another change in the management so quickly. Most everyone in the industry knew the gossip about the internal problems of the D&RG. Luke didn't know any details; only that Palmer had been voted out by the stockholders, and then the company folded. Luke felt that it served them right to have the company go bankrupt after removing the General.

David Moffat also took a moment to size up Luke. Colonel Ballister was, without question, a railroad man. His hands were red and calloused, and his nails hadn't been cleaned recently. There was no shame in that. But he didn't wish to shake his hand. For the sake of hygiene, as well as other reasons. Hints of thick muscle showed at Ballister's neck and wrists. His skin had a tanned, leathery appearance that told of countless hours toiling in the sun. He knew the muscles had been honed by years of hard labor, building roads. Moffat was interested in railroads — but in the profits they raised, not the work in the field. "I'm sure you're wondering why we've called you here, Colonel," began Jackson.

Luke thought about asking the men to call him by his Christian name, then decided against it. These older men were presently treating him as an equal, due to his war rank. So be it. "I must profess to a certain amount of curiosity," Luke agreed with a nod. "The General's cable was somewhat vague."

William Jackson gestured with a hand, offering Luke a chair. Suddenly Luke felt the urge to brush off his clothing before sitting. He knew it was silly. These were both railroad men. Surely they understood road dust.

Jackson sat down only after Luke had, then fixed Luke with a piercing stare. Luke crossed one leg over the other so that his left boot rested on his right knee. Might as well be comfortable.

"Have you ever been to the Grand Cañon of the Grand[1], Colonel?" asked Jackson in a rolling rumble.

"I know where it is, but I've never been there," Luke replied. "I was on the crew that took the road to Red Cliff in '83, but General Palmer decided that the canyon couldn't be breached, and the rails were abandoned."

"Actually," Moffat interjected, "that's not accurate. The road was abandoned because the company was nearly bankrupt, not because the job couldn't be done. If Palmer hadn't overspent, we'd already be hauling coal and silver from the valley."

Moffat watched stubborn, angry lines set in Ballister's face. He didn't care. Those were the facts. He'd been faced with cleaning up Palmer's mess and trying to hold together the fragile pieces of the D&RG. General Palmer had not managed the company properly. He had no concept of fiscal responsibility. Palmer had laid over one thousand miles of new rail in only a few years, spending millions upon millions of dollars. He laid more line than the population of Colorado had ever dreamed possible. If there was a town, Palmer wanted to reach it. He had a vision, and visions aren't cheap.

But millions were spent by other railroads, as well. Suddenly, the Baby Road was competing with the likes of the Union Pacific and Atchison's group out of Kansas. With cheap, available transportation from multiple sources, the public demanded, and received, lower and lower fares. Goods could be moved more cheaply as well. Suddenly, income from freight was reduced to the point that interest on the bonds could not be paid.

Then came the lawsuits. Soon they couldn't even pay wages. Far in debt, and forced into bankruptcy, the Board quietly removed Palmer and agreed to allow a receiver to protect the assets. Hard decisions had to be made in '84. Construction, except for repairs, stopped. Workers found employment elsewhere. It had made Moffat both sad and angry. He knew many men had followed Palmer's vision blindly. For a time he had been one of them. This Ballister fellow was another. It was a fanatic sort of loyalty that would overlook every fault, refusing to believe until it was too late.

Luke held his temper. He already knew he didn't like Moffat. There was something about the man that was condescending. His voice was cold steel when he responded, but he was polite. "All I know is the General told me it wasn't cost effective to go through the canyon. I trust him in matters of money."

Moffat snorted lightly and didn't shrink from Luke's angry look. "So did we, Colonel. So did we."

Jackson watched the rising level of animosity between the two men with sympathy toward them both. He knew that Palmer had overspent, but also knew that Palmer was right to have done it. Last October, Jackson had written an open letter to the Baby Road's investors in London. He told them that the D&RG must either assert their ownership of the abandoned Red Cliff road, the gateway to Aspen, and fight for it, or quietly abandon it. He said that the D&RG could not afford not to build. If the road did not occupy the Grand Valley with a line, some other company would. Jackson understood the irony: they were now fighting one final time for Palmer's vision. In 1884, Palmer had tried to convince the Board of Directors in New York that the road must be taken to Aspen. It was the last step, he claimed, to connecting the riches of Aspen's silver mines and the Grand Valley's abundant coal deposits with Denver and Salt Lake City. The board had refused. On his way out the door, Palmer warned that they were making a fatal mistake.

It had been hard for Jackson and Moffat to admit that Palmer had been right in his predictions. Without the revenues from hauling the silver and coal ore from the Roaring Fork Valley, the Baby Road would perish. Now nearly three years later, they were obliged to complete the line to Aspen. They knew Palmer was laughing at them.

The most urgent concern in the minds of Jackson and Moffat was a new upstart local road, the Colorado Midland, based out of Colorado Springs. Small but well funded, it was a potential threat to the ailing D&RG. The Midland had surprised everyone when they found a back route to Aspen. Over a new pass they called Hagerman, named for the owner of the Midland, they stood to reach Aspen in less than a year. Even broke, the Board realized they had no choice but to build or perish. The investors couldn't decide. The decision was tabled month after month. So, without their permission, the Board agreed to build. Without permission they hired crews. But they were losing the race. Now, without permission, they were about to hire Colonel Ballister. It was a gamble, and the odds were against them.

Moffat and Ballister continued to stare at each other with rising levels of animosity, until Jackson intervened.

"Regardless, gentlemen, of the reason why the road was abandoned, we are now embarking on a plan to complete the line. In October of last year we began to lay down track from the Red Cliff station. Last Friday our crews reached the eastern edge of the Cañon. Over one thousand men are working, as we speak, to build a combination narrow and standard gauge bed through solid rock. We have less than six months to reach Aspen or we'll lose everything."

Jackson stared at Luke until he was certain he had the man's full attention. "Our purpose today is to ask whether you would be willing to take over as head of the project."

# CHAPTER 3

Luke was stunned. Truly stunned. He could think of no words to say to Jackson's request. A thousand men. A wild cañon that had never been crossed. Luke tried to give the impression of thoughtful silence, rather than the heart-pounding terror he actually felt.

"Obviously, I'll need to know the answers to several questions before I make that decision," was what finally came out of his mouth. He saw both of the men brighten slightly.

"We'll answer anything we can," Moffat said.

A hundred questions fought for space in Luke's head. The question which finally slipped out of his throat was, "Who's leading the project now?"

"That is immaterial," replied Moffat quickly. Luke's eyes narrowed. Not to him, it wasn't! He needed to know what sort of situation he would be heading into, *if* he agreed to the job.

Luke pressed on. "Did he quit? Is he dead?"

Jackson responded this time. "You will be replacing him. That's all you need to know."

So the present boss was being fired, or reassigned. That information was valuable. It led to his next question.

"Why me?" It was the question he had intended to ask first. "I've never worked for either of you. Hellfire, I wasn't even a gang boss under General Palmer. What makes you think I can do this?"

The corner of David Moffat's mouth turned up in amusement. "Palmer said you were direct," he commented.

William Jackson explained. "The General did recommend you," he began, "but we talked with many people before we decided to offer the job to you. I personally spoke with several of your previous supervisors, as well as men from this and other roads who have worked with and under you. All of the information gathered leads to the conclusion that you have a high level of command ability. You're personally driven, intensely honest, a perfectionist, and are dedicated to the road. All of those qualities are needed in this position. In addition, you have the reputation for being able to ramrod a crew. With the time constraints we are under, that quality alone is worth the offer." He paused and his eyes locked with Luke's for a moment. "Does that answer your question?"

It did, and Luke nodded thoughtfully. Several points that Jackson raised, however, concerned Luke. He decided to be blunt. He leaned back in his chair and interlocked his fingers. He split his attention between the two men, and spoke.

"I think at this point I need to make you aware of a few facts. First, if I've gotten the reputation for ramrodding a crew, I'm sorry. I don't ramrod men." He waited for a moment to let that sink in. The two interviewers exchanged glances, but Luke continued before they could voice any questions.

"I do insist that the men under me work to the best of their ability. I have high expectations, but I'm hardly a perfectionist. Perfection isn't always possible in the field. There are always trade-offs. Sometimes production is more important, and sometimes common sense is." Luke wanted to make certain they understood how he managed men. They may decide he wasn't fit for the job. Better to find out now than when it was too late.

"I know there are gang bosses who use threats and violence to increase production," he continued. He vividly remembered some of the more sadistic bosses he had been unfortunate enough to be assigned to in the past. "I had enough blood and pain in the war. I'll fire a man before I'll beat him. My crews had high production because they *wanted* to be there. I don't want to work with anyone who doesn't want to perform. It wastes my time and theirs. I will direct and focus my crew, but I can't lead anyone who won't follow. If you consider that ramrodding, then so be it."

Luke paused for a breath. He considered asking for a drink of water, but didn't want to interrupt the flow. He was now earnestly considering accepting the job, sight unseen. He liked a challenge. But there were still a number of issues.

He continued very seriously, making sure he had both men's attention. "If I take this on, I'll likely fire a number of people right off. Possibly, a great number. At first, there might be a drop in production. But once the deadwood is gone, it'll actually increase the speed of the job. I'd also like the authority to determine wages. Good money will keep the best people working hard. An end bonus would be acceptable. Won't lose as many people when the firings start. Finally, I don't want to be second-guessed every moment. Because of the location, I'll need your authority behind me to make decisions in situations where I won't have time to involve you." Luke had learned only recently that unless it was agreed up front to let him manage, somebody over him in another location would think he knew better than Luke, even though Luke was right there involved in the mess.

"Now," he concluded, "if you're still interested in me after knowing all that, then I have several more specific questions."

Moffat found himself leaning forward in his chair, intently interested. He had watched the flashing eyes and determination of this man as he spoke his mind. Moffat was impressed, despite his own misgivings. He understood instantly why Palmer had recommended Ballister. He was a little surprised Palmer hadn't tried to slip them an incompetent. Moffat was loathe to admit that he had prejudices against friends of Palmer's without even meeting them.

Jackson's smile started slowly and spread, stretching his coarse, white chin hair. "What you just said, Colonel, was *exactly* what I was hoping to hear. As far as I'm concerned, the job is yours. Any argument, David?" he asked his replacement.

Moffat nodded his head with pursed lips. "It's possible that the crew needs a little shaking up. I haven't been to the site personally, but there are problems." An ironic smile turned up one corner of his mouth. "So let's turn the tables and see if the *Colonel* is still interested once we explain the situation."

# CHAPTER 4

Moffat and Jackson looked at each other, deciding who would begin the tale. There were many things to discuss, but some things were not the concern of the potential gang boss. These matters concerned politics between the Baby Road and the Midland, and also with the Western, Palmer's company in Salt Lake City. The two men had decided earlier to only discuss the situation in the Cañon. The rest was their affair.

"The Grand River Cañon," began Jackson, "is a geologic masterpiece — and a geologic nightmare. The walls are 2,000 feet vertical from the river's edge to the top. The composition is a combination of granite, sandstone and limestone, in horizontal layers, some as thick as ten feet, or as thin as six inches. We're building on the south face of the canyon, at a level which is mostly granite. In some parts, there's a natural shelf which could be utilized. Unfortunately, the grade varies wildly from one shelf to another. In order for a loaded engine to scale it, the final grade must be no more than two percent, although we are trying to achieve a one percent grade. We're also completing four tunnels. A blasting crew has been working ahead of the main group to even the incline and create the tunnels. Naturally, blasting is especially difficult with the different veins of rock."

Luke nodded. He had briefly been part of a blasting crew while bringing the road to Red Cliff. The rock strata was especially difficult to control. The granite took a large blast to break up but smoothed right out. The sandstone only needed a gentle tap but then couldn't be stabilized. Mix in the crumbly limestone and only the best pyrotechnicians could handle the job.

"I presume you have Chinese crews doing that part?" he asked. "Most of the best dynamiters I've known have been Celestials."

Jackson nodded. "We've tried other crews, but the Chinese are the most efficient. Plus, they request the assignments, regardless of the danger. And there is danger. There was a severe flood in '85, and most of the vegetation and animals in the canyon were lost. The high waters de-stabilized the formation well above the water line, and there are continuing landslides. Surveying has been difficult. The crews will finish in one location, only to have the wall break apart and fall into the river before the blasters can reach it, and then it has to be surveyed all over again. Two months ago, we lost almost an entire survey crew in a slide." He let that sink into Luke's mind.

Moffat chimed in, changing the subject slightly. "To our benefit, the cañon seems to be in a weather vortex. The temperatures are mild throughout the year, and there's little snow. That has been in our favor. The Midland is working at nearly 10,000 feet, going over Hagerman Pass. They've been moving slowly because of the hard winter. However, they are now on the downslope, and with spring melting the snows, they'll soon begin to increase their speed. Our informants indicate that, given their current speed, they'll reach Aspen before Christmas. We intend to beat them."

"I've heard rumors that the Union Pacific is interested in the Roaring Fork Valley too," Luke commented. "Any truth to the gossip?"

Moffat and Jackson glanced at each other. They had heard that particular gossip and had verified that the rumors were true, but they weren't aware it was common knowledge. "Where did you get this information?"

Luke shrugged. "Talk, here and there. The race between you and the Midland is fairly well known right now. It wouldn't surprise me for the UP to wonder what the fuss was about and stick in their oar."

What worried Moffat and Jackson more than the UP's interest in Aspen's mines were the rumors that they were interested in purchasing the Midland. The D&RG could not win a battle with the UP right now. They were having enough trouble with Atchison's group breaking the Treaty of Boston. Hearing that the UP's intrusion was common knowledge only made Moffat more determined to reach Aspen first.

"How long is the canyon?" Luke asked after a moment.

"Nearly thirteen miles," Jackson replied. "Thirteen miles of working on a rock shelf barely wide enough to fit ten men across. At times, the shelf is nearly twenty feet above the river."

Luke furrowed his brow at that. "How do you get supplies to the crews? Where's the camp?"

Jackson reached into a corner and picked up a rolled sheet of thick paper. He untied the faded red ribbon that bound it and spread it on the nearly empty desk.

Luke picked up a heavy crystal paperweight that was shaped like a steam engine and put it on one corner of the paper. The paperweight had always been a favorite of Palmer's, and Luke wondered why he'd left it behind. Suddenly, he had a flash of memory of sitting in this same spot with Palmer opening another print of an earlier line. General

Palmer was grinning because he had just signed the papers with investors that would allow him to build out the print.

Then came a second flash of remembrance, this time of a train in Pennsylvania. And of General Palmer, grinning at a young Colonel Ballister, covered in soot and a week's worth of sweat.

Luke was a minor officer, a lieutenant first class under General Sherman, during his famed "march to the sea." Luke had received a field promotion for "bravery" during the Battle of Shiloh. Fool luck and fear were often seen as bravery, after the fact.

Most people thought that General Sherman was brave, too. Pushing into enemy territory, slashing and burning his way to Atlanta. Truth be told, General Sherman had no *choice* but to move forward. He was out of supplies for his troops. Every mile they progressed was another mile of foodstuffs for his hungry men. Luke understood the difficult decision Sherman had made. Retreat and maybe lose the war, or proceed and maybe lose his men to slaughter. Perhaps *that* was the brave part. The decision itself.

Luke had received his lieutenant's stripes at the tender age of fifteen. He had been only twelve years old when Confederate troops invaded his family's Virginia farm. They decided his home was a good base. They had killed his parents, and raped his sister. Then they shot her. Luke had been out hunting when the soldiers came, and watched from a distance as his family was executed. Driven by anger and hate, he ran — far from Virginia. He lied about his age and joined the Union Army. The faces of the soldiers who killed his family were burned into his mind. He took great pleasure in tracking down the men, and shooting them, one at a time. His fellows helped, after Luke told them the story. It was personal for him, as it was for many. The Civil War was very personal. It started for beliefs, but then it became personal. It was a side of himself Luke wasn't fond of. So he was Mister Ballister now. War hero or not.

It seemed fated for Luke to become a hero one summer day when he and two other men captured, by accident, a Confederate train engine with two cars attached. General Sherman had pulled him aside after Luke presented him with the prize. The General ordered Luke to take the train north to General Palmer's camp somewhere in Pennsylvania and bring back food and ammo. General Palmer's Fifteenth Pennsylvania Volunteer Calvary was responsible for tearing up Confederate track to remove the enemy's ability to resupply. Where there was track, Luke would find Palmer.

General Sherman had given Luke a written message for General Palmer, and instructed him to deliver it *only* to Palmer. Luke had been nervous about the assignment. He had been on a train before. That was how he got north from his ruined home in Virginia to join the Union forces. Trouble was, he had never *driven* one before.

It had been an experience. He, Carl, Elias, and Matthew managed to figure out all the levers and knobs, and make the train move forward. They figured out how to run the boiler — eventually. They even managed not to wreck the train while they were learning these things. Luke couldn't explain his lack of knowledge to General Sherman. Sherman didn't want excuses. If he ordered you to do something, he expected you to do it, whether or not you knew *how*.

As Luke and the three men boarded the train, he had turned to the General and said with a snap salute, "I'll get the train there, sir!"

There was a brief moment when Luke could have sworn that there was a sparkle of amusement in the General's eyes. He replied, very seriously, "I'm sure you will, *Colonel* Ballister."

Luke's eyes went wide as he stood at the rail of the reverberating engine, but his salute never wavered. At first, he thought he might have heard the General wrong, because of the noise from the train. But then he saw the men under him look at each other in surprise. A second promotion in less than a year! *And* he'd skipped three grades!

The General returned his salute, and then added, "Make sure you bring the train *back*, as well."

Luke tried very hard not to smile. "Yes, Sir!" he responded.

They found Palmer's makeshift camp many days later, where the rails disappeared from sabotage. There was black soot and sweat caked on their uniforms and on any skin open to air. His squad was angry when they weren't well received. But Luke tried to imagine how he would treat four dirty, sweaty men riding on a Confederate engine into Sherman's camp. Probably the same. He sighed.

He had raised his hands when the guns pointed at them, and ordered his men to lay down their arms.

"We need to see General Palmer," Luke told the man who appeared to be the leader.

The collected men laughed as though Luke had just told a joke. "I'm sure you do, boy." replied the leader, who wore lieutenant stripes. "And even if you ain't Confederate spies, which we haven't rightly decided, the General ain't got no time to talk to a wet-eared kid."

Luke ignored the 'kid' remark. It was understandable. There was no sense antagonizing these men. They were all on the same side.

"I need to reach inside my jacket," warned Luke. "Don't get excited." Luke put one arm down to reach into his uniform. The men moved nervously, but nobody fired at him. He removed the paper with General Sherman's personal seal embossed in heavy red wax. "This is an important message from General Sherman. I have to deliver it to General Palmer."

The Lieutenant looked at him for a long moment, then put down his weapon. He walked to the edge of the engine, and reached out his hand. "I'll give it to him, boy."

Luke pulled the paper back out of reach. "I am supposed to deliver it *only* to General Palmer."

A voice came from his right, and Luke turned his head. The crowd had parted to allow a smallish man to walk through. He walked with a confidence, a strength, that told Luke immediately who he was.

"I'm Palmer," the man said.

"General Palmer, Sir!" Luke said, and he and his men, dirty and tired as they were, fell into snap attention. Even the churlish Lieutenant went to attention. Luke saluted smartly.

General Palmer returned the salute, looked at the engine, and then looked at Luke with a healthy dose of suspicion.

"Boy," he said to Luke, "Where did you get this train?"

Luke thought of a hundred responses, but all of them were too long. He had the feeling that Palmer wanted a short, simple answer. Luke glanced at the General, then stared straight ahead, like a disciplined soldier.

"We borrowed it, Sir!"

There was silence. When Luke risked a glance at the General, the man's face was split with a smile from ear to ear and his chest was moving lightly in a quiet chuckle. Luke took that as a good sign. He reached out and handed the message to the General.

"This is from General Sherman, Sir!" Then he returned to attention.

General Palmer opened the wax seal and read the message. His eyebrows raised until one disappeared under his unruly hair. "Well, *Colonel* Ballister, welcome to my camp." Luke could see the surprised looks on the faces of the much older men, not a stripe among them, who still held guns trained on them. "You men start loading whatever supplies we can spare on this train." The guns lowered and they hurried to obey.

Then Palmer turned to the surly Lieutenant, and said in a voice of reprimand, "Lieutenant, show the Colonel where he and his men can clean up. *Your* tent will do, I think." He turned to Luke. "I look forward to speaking with you, Colonel, about the situation to the south. I hope you'll join me for dinner."

That was the beginning of a long friendship between the two men. Now, here he was, twenty-three years later, nearly forty years old, feeling like a kid again. And on a new project — one that Palmer had a hand in planning.

Jackson's finger on the print brought Luke back to the present. "Here's the main camp, at the east edge of the cañon. This is Dot Zero."

Luke stared at the print. It gave no indication of the task ahead. It showed the route, nothing more. The cañon walls were etched in, but there was no scale that could be relied on for his purposes.

Luke spent the day in the office, learning every detail he cared to know about the project itself, and almost nothing at all about the men he would lead. Each time he tried to ask specific questions about why production had slowed, the two men hedged, or changed the subject back to the technical details.

After hours of trying to get a story, he made a decision. "I'm interested in the job, gentlemen, but I'm a little skittish about accepting it before I have a chance to look it over. It might be more than I'm capable of. So, I'll make you a deal, if you're willing."

Jackson and Moffat glanced at each other curiously, and then looked back to Luke. "What are you proposing?"

"I'd like to work on the survey crew for a day or two — however long the next pay train normally stays there before returning. As a surveyor foreman, I can move from camp to camp, taking the temperature of the project. Introduce me to the head paymaster — provided his honesty is above reproach — and tell him who I am. Other than him, I don't want a general announcement. I won't get the straight story if people know who I am. Folks'll be too busy making a good impression. Give the paymaster a letter from you to the present gang boss stating that he is to return to Denver on the train. It is only to be delivered if I accept the job. I'll seek out the paymaster on my own before they leave, either to get passage back to Denver, or to accept the job. Is that fair?"

Jackson tapped his finger on the print, thinking the offer through. David Moffat sat down in his chair once more. Minor annoyance played across his face.

"We had hoped to secure either a yes or no before you left, Colonel," Jackson said truthfully.

"I can appreciate that," Luke replied. "However, it seems that neither of you is fully familiar with why the project is going sour. There's no fault in that. People probably haven't been square with you, or they don't know. I don't know that I can fix things, so I need to see for myself what *is* wrong. It's only a day or two more. If I don't take the job, at least there'll be no lapse in production."

Moffat nodded suddenly. "I agree. Let him see the job. We shouldn't be afraid of what he'll find."

The attitude, from David Moffat, surprised Luke. Maybe there was more to the man than he thought. Maybe he could come to respect him.

"Very well," Jackson said. "I'll dictate the letter to Mr. Carpenter right now. The next pay train leaves the Denver station tomorrow morning. I'll introduce you to the head paymaster, Jarrod Talbot." He stopped for a moment, and then spoke. "In addition to introducing you in person, I will draft a letter of introduction, in case Jarrod's word is questioned. If you decide to accept the job, please send a cable through Gypsum. You will report only to me and, upon my departure, to Mr. Moffat. Be at the station at 6:00 A.M. sharp." He raised his voice slightly. "Joshua! Please come in here."

Luke stood and shook both men's hands. "I do look forward to working with you both. It sounds like an interesting race. I hope I'll be a part of it."

As he shook Jackson's hand, the older man smiled. "Before you leave, Colonel, aren't you at all curious about the pay?"

Luke returned the smile. "I presume that my pay will be based on the difficulty of the job, and the speed in which you wish it done."

"Well said, Colonel. We're presently paying $200 per month. The two hundred for this meeting is a small bonus, in anticipation of success." Luke's eyebrows shot up onto his forehead. Two hundred a *month*? They really were in a hurry!

William opened the center drawer of the heavy oak desk and removed a stack of green paper. "The second half of your two hundred, Colonel. I hope this money was well spent."

Luke accepted the money as the clerk, Joshua Anderson, opened the paneled oak door on oiled hinges.

Moffat spoke, "We've arranged for a room for you two blocks down at The Hotel Larimer. The room isn't fancy, but it's comfortable. Enjoy your evening. Mr. Jackson will meet you in the morning. I have a business meeting, and won't be able to attend."

"Gentlemen, it's been a pleasure," Luke said as he took his leave. He picked up his coat and hat in the front room, and noticed out the window that the rain had turned to snow. His horse, Star, would be miserable by now. He'd make sure she was stabled for the night. He would have to make arrangements for boarding her. She was a fine quarter horse, but she wasn't a proper mount for a cañon. He presumed there would be sure-footed mules at his new job.

A new job. It seemed almost certain to him at this point. Six months or more at two hundred dollars a month! Plus, he saw the dotted line on the print he was shown. The next spur had already been planned to connect Aspen with Grand Junction. Maybe he'd be able to run that job, as well. He'd heard Grand Junction was a good place to settle down.

But settling down was for later. Now there was a cañon to tame!

# CHAPTER 5

Morning came quicker than Luke would have liked. He had spent his evening in Denver cleaning up and getting business settled. He arranged for Star to be boarded, and spent some time at a bath house. He had the money to buy all the extras for a change. He stopped by a clothier's and purchased a few things for a long stay outside of civilization — union suits and wool stockings, plus a new pair of boots. It was probably still winter in the cañon. By the time it was warm enough for a single pair of stockings, the new boots would be broken in.

Most men didn't consider a razor and soap necessities, but Luke did. A beard was fine for the winter, but he preferred to be clean shaven. And he was as persnickety as the Celestials about daily bathing. He opened an account at the local bank. He would try to make arrangements to have his pay deposited directly to the account. He didn't want to have that much money in his possession every month. It would just be asking for trouble.

Finally, Luke had a thick steak with potatoes for dinner, with fresh apple pie for dessert. At the end of the day he got a real luxury — sleeping on a soft bed with clean sheets. He didn't get a chance to do that often, and he always appreciated it.

Luke had all of his gear packed and was waiting at the station by 5:50 the next morning. The morning was crisp, but warmer than Luke had expected. The snow from the night before had melted on the cobblestones surrounding the elegant brick train station. He could barely see his breath when he exhaled. The eastern sky was fading from a rich velvet blue to gold as Luke watched over the top of the brick arch that proclaimed its welcome to visitors arriving at the Union Station. Steam from the warming engine hovered in the air around him. The rising sun turned the steam rich reds and oranges to match the sky. Luke moved to the edge of the station house to look at the mountains to the west. The sun glinted off the distant peaks, making the remaining snow appear lavishly golden. There were few things more beautiful than the rising sun in Colorado. He had been many places in his life, but here was where he intended to stay.

Ominous dark clouds poked over the tops of the peaks. Somewhere in those mountains, it was snowing. Luke frowned briefly. It would be just his luck to have it be where he was headed.

Six o'clock came and went as Luke waited. His gear was neatly packed in a duffel bag at his feet. He watched the activity of the crews loading the cars and waited for Jackson to arrive. Men began to appear at the edge of the track where the train was building steam. Two men who obviously worked for the road set up a table near the entrance to the building with a placard that read, "Denver & Rio Grande — sign up here." A line formed as Luke watched. He decided to wait for Jackson rather than introduce himself. One by one the men approached the table, made their mark on a paper, and were directed where to board the train. Most did not board immediately. They found others like themselves, and huddled in groups, chatting. Luke was amazed at the mix of men he was going to command. Chinese in ponytails wore that curious design of shirt with the high neck and wide, flowing sleeves. Mexicans wore thick, long moustaches and had dark skin. There were Irish gandydancers with dark or red hair and freckles scattered across smiling faces, and even a few Negroes, muscles threatening to rip through homespun shirts. Luke had worked with some of the men before, although he didn't know their names. He didn't notice anyone in particular that might pose a problem to the job. He always made a point to remember the troublemakers from previous jobs, men who had been run off for stealing or who were hitchers. Hitchers annoyed Luke the most. They signed on just to get a ride to wherever the job was, then deserted with the equipment that had been assigned to them, leaving the crew shorthanded and without enough tools.

It was nearly 6:30 when he saw Jackson's tall form walking down Blake Street toward the station. He was walking slowly, leaning heavily on a cane. It was hard for Luke to remain angry, remembering the toll that the full day meeting yesterday took on the man.

"Good morning, Mr. Jackson," Luke said when he was close enough to hear.

"I apologize for keeping you waiting, Colonel," Jackson replied. "I'm afraid this old body doesn't move quite as quickly as it used to."

"It was no trouble," Luke said graciously. "I've spent the time looking around. I believe they're almost ready to leave." He directed Jackson's attention to where the table was being removed, and the workers were boarding.

"Just so," Jackson replied, and walked a little faster toward the entrance. "Jarrod!" he called to the two men. One of the men turned, and Luke got a long look at him.

Jarrod Talbot was under six feet, and had a medium build. He wore a standard cotton shirt and well-worn, but clean, work pants.

His heavy leather coat had been exposed to many years of elements. As he approached the pair, Luke noticed he had a rough scar down one cheek. It almost looked like a lash mark.

Jarrod was beaming a surprised smile, and held out his hand to the older gentleman. "William Jackson, you old reprobate! It's been a long time. How are the fancy offices treating you?"

Jackson had to change the cane he was holding to his left hand in order to offer Talbot his right. He shook the younger man's hand firmly, and replied, "I'm about to be put out to pasture, I'm afraid. The doctor told me I have to slow down a bit. Running a road is a game for the young."

Jarrod's broad face looked surprised. "You're retiring? After that bear grip you just gave me, I would have thought you were in perfect health."

Jackson chuckled. "That's kind of you, Jarrod." He turned his head to look at Luke. "Jarrod, I'd like you to meet Colonel Luke Ballister. Colonel, Jarrod Talbot." The two men shook hands.

"Any friend of Will's is a friend of mine," said Jarrod. "Are you this old scoundrel's replacement?"

Luke gave a surprised laugh. "Hardly!" He glanced at Jackson to see whether he should introduce himself. Jackson didn't give him the chance.

"No, Jarrod. Luke is, and this is confidential — only between us — going to be taking over as the gang boss for the Aspen project."

Jarrod's eyes went wide. "I can't say I'm surprised you're replacing Carpenter, Will. Frankly, I hope he hasn't already wrecked your chances." He turned to Luke. "You ever been a boss before, Colonel?"

Luke nodded. "Please call me Luke. And yes, I just finished running the line to Pueblo for the AT. This will probably be the *biggest* job I've ever run, though."

Jarrod shook his head with a weary smile. "Well, glad to see you're back on our side. But if you haven't stopped into the local druggist, I suggest you do, and stock up on headache powder. You'll need it."

Luke took the comment under consideration as Jackson continued. He reached into his inner jacket pocket, and removed two folded letters. "Jarrod, I want you to hold on to these letters. One is to Carpenter, instructing him to return to Denver for re-assignment. The other is a letter of introduction for the Colonel. The Colonel hasn't quite decided whether to join us, and wants to look over the site beforehand. I want you to mark him on your logs as being a temporary surveyor foreman, assigned to review the work against the prints. He'll wander the camps and look things over. Make sure he finds you before you head back here. He'll either ride back with you, if he doesn't want the job, or ask you to deliver the letters. I know it's a lot to ask, Jarrod," said the older man, settling a solid hand on Talbot's shoulder. "I'm certain Carpenter won't leave quietly."

"No, he probably won't." Jarrod turned to Luke, and added, "I hope you can handle yourself, Colonel. There's likely to be a fight. Carpenter's got his own men firmly installed under him, and they'll fight for him. It could get ugly."

Luke pursed his lips. "What about your men?" he asked. "Will they back me up against Carpenter?"

Jarrod shook his head thoughtfully. "If they heard it from you, Will, probably. Just on my say-so, though? I don't know. I think we'll have to tell them. I understand the risk of the word getting out, but there just isn't any choice."

"Colonel?" asked Jackson with a significance Luke recognized. He wanted Luke to decide whether to risk too many people having knowledge of the plan. As much as he would like to remain under cover, Luke recognized strength in numbers. If the change in command was truly going to be a problem, he needed as many friends as he could get. He gave a brief nod, and Jarrod quickly left to fetch the rest of the payroll guards and the engine staff.

When the staff was assembled, Jackson explained the situation. Almost all of the men nodded in agreement, understanding their role immediately. When he had finished, and had stressed the need for confidence, he asked, "Does anyone have any questions?"

One man who stood in the back raised his hand. Jarrod looked at him and asked, "Yeah, Ben? You got a question?"

"I ain't got no question," replied Ben with a thick Southern accent. He wore a heavy cloth coat and a Stetson pulled down low over angry eyes. He had a rifle stock in one hand. The barrel rested over the opposite forearm. "But I won't guard the back of that murderous son-of-a-bitch!"

Luke furrowed his brow, trying to remember if he had ever met the man. As far as he could remember, he hadn't.

"What are you talking about, Ben?" asked Jarrod, confused and annoyed.

Ben pointed a long finger at Luke. "That damn Bluebelly was with Sherman when he burned down my family's farm. Didn't even leave us enough to eat for the winter. My baby sister died 'cause there wasn't no food. I remember the faces of those men. He was one of the leaders. Sitting there on his white horse, shouting orders to burn our fields. No, sir! I won't watch his back. You can fire me if you will. I don't like Carpenter any better than anyone, Jarrod, and I got no quarrel with you or the other boys iffen you want to back him, but I just can't."

"Ben, the war's been over for years! You can't hold things that happened twenty years ago against a person."

"Maybe you can't, Jarrod. But my sister would have been a growed woman by now. Broke my Mama's heart to bury her." The man was nearly shaking, but his face gave nothing away. He shook his head. "Nope. My mind's made up. I've been with the road for a long time, but I can't do this. I'll give the man his pay, but I won't fight for him."

"Ben! You're being . . .," began Jarrod.

Luke held up his hand. "No, Jarrod. I won't force a man to back me." He addressed the stricken man directly. "Sir, I'm sorry if I was involved in the death of your sister. I truly am. I can't make up for my actions during the war. It was a war, and hard things were decided. But I can apologize for them. I won't ask you to forgive me, because there are things *I* can't forgive, either. But I have to know whether you'll break the confidence Mr. Jackson has asked for, or whether you'll side with Carpenter in a fight. I won't ask you men to stand against each other. That alone was the hardest part of the war. Friends standing against each other. I won't be party to that."

The dozen men turned their attention to their friend. One of the other men spoke. "Ben, we've been friends for years. I was on the Union side, too. You've known that. Zeke, here, marched under the Confederate flag. I thought we had gotten past where we came from."

"I thought I had, too, Matthew. I thought I had, too." Then he turned and walked away from the group, away from the train, and entered the station.

Jarrod addressed Jackson. "I'll talk to him, Will. He'll be fine." He turned and started to follow the other man.

"No, Jarrod, I'll talk to him myself. You men need to get started. I can't risk the whole project for one man's problems. Can you deliver the payroll short a man?"

A man wearing conductor's garb spoke up. "I can handle a gun well enough, Mr. Jackson. I can take Ben's place. I was born here in Colorado territory. I didn't take no sides in the war, and I'll be pleased as punch to throw Carpenter out on his ear." A few men gave a nervous chuckle.

Jackson nodded his agreement. "Anyone else have a problem?"

There were a few shakes, and a few shrugs, but no other objections. "Very well, then," concluded Jackson. "I wish you all well." He shook each man's hand, to the surprise of the guards, and then turned and walked toward the station.

"All right, then," Jarrod said, "Let's hit the road, boys." He turned to Luke and added, "If you want to sit with me, I can bring you up to date."

Luke considered the offer, then shook his head. "Thank you, but I don't want to set myself apart from the others if I can avoid it. I need to get the scuttlebutt from the workers. I'll need some prints to look over, though, if I hope to appear to know what I'm doing when I arrive."

"We've got some grade prints in the tool car," Jarrod said as they walked toward the train.

Jarrod swung up onto the tool car, located directly behind the coal tinder, and emerged moments later with several sets of rolled prints. Luke accepted them gratefully, and climbed the stairs onto the lead passenger car.

Over twenty men watched Luke enter the car. They seemed to sense something different about him. He was no ordinary rust eater. He carried blueprints. Maybe a foreman? Luke seated himself in an unoccupied seat facing the rear of the train and waited for the trip to begin.

A piercing whistle cut the air, and the characteristic thrum began to sound from the engine. Black smoke rolled past the window nearest Luke, as the winds from the approaching storm pushed the air toward the ground. The train lurched abruptly, and Luke was moved forward in his seat. Several more lurches followed before the train picked up enough speed to smooth out the ride. Luke never failed to be excited about a train journey. Soon, he knew, rails would span the continent and any person could travel from New York to California in just a few short days. It was a changing world and he wanted to be part of it.

# CHAPTER 6

Edward O'Malley heard the supper chime sound, and stopped his sledge in mid-swing. After setting the hammer on the ground, he stretched his massive back muscles this way and that, easing the tension. The raw wounds on his back protested sharply with the movement, but Edward was growing accustomed to them. His shaggy hair had slipped out of the leather thong which bound it. He took a moment to tie it back out of his eyes. The air in the cañon was still for a change. He looked up to see heavy clouds forming overhead. Another spring storm. No matter. He was accustomed to them.

Edward took a deep breath of the stale, dusty air, and wandered toward the kitchen car to pick up his dinner pail.

He nodded greetings to others in the crew and they returned his nods. An O'Toole here, and a Coughlin there. Some were friends, others family members, but they hardly spoke anymore. It felt like they had forgotten how. Speaking while working wasn't allowed. After the most recent round of lashes, Edward was working hard to remember that lesson.

He could smell the cooked food as he approached the rail car. Beans again. And probably chicory to drink. Oh, what he wouldn't give for a hearty swallow of fine Irish whiskey and a bowl of Maggie's thick lamb stew. It had been nearly five months since he'd had a taste of red meat. He found it hard to imagine the railroad was so broke it couldn't afford the cost of a few sheep on occasion.

He waited in line with the others, and accepted the tin pail filled with lukewarm beans. A small piece of sourdough hardtack rested on top of the beans and soaked up the rich sauce. Barely enough to keep a man alive, he thought.

Edward found a rock to perch on. He glanced around the landscape as he ate. Snow still covered the top of the ridge, and bits of white dusted high ledges of stone. A movement caught his eye. After searching he finally spotted a large ram, nearly identical in color to the surrounding rock. It balanced on a small outcropping of rock that shouldn't have been able to hold the animal's weight. It gazed down at him with calm black eyes. Yet another of the strange animals in this cañon. There were bright yellow fish in the water with pink flesh. Others had humps on their backs like they were unfinished by the creator. Large cats, longer than he was tall, roamed the rocky depths. The cats' cries were piercing screeches that set his teeth on edge.

He marveled at huge pine trees jutting out from solid rock, suspended in mid-air a thousand feet above his head. They somehow withstood wind and weather, looking both delicate and sturdy at the same time.

A young boy passed him, on his way to another boulder to sit.

"Tommy O'Rourke!" he said softly and the boy turned to his voice. He raised his eyebrows in question.

"Come sit by me, boyo," Edward said, a command frilling the edges of the words.

The boy began to look nervous, but obeyed.

"Yes, Edward?" he asked, as he sat in the space the older man made for him on the large flat rock.

Edward's voice dropped to a whisper, but the rolling Irish accent remained. "And didn't I just see ye passing by only a moment ago with a tin of food?"

A quick smile passed over Tommy's face and he had the good grace to blush. The freckles on his young face stood out in dark relief against the red. "Aye, that you did," he replied in a similar whisper.

Edward let out an exasperated breath. "Jesus, Mary and Joseph, boyo. Are ye daft!?! They'll put the whip to ye for that. Stealing, they call it."

Tommy's face set in tight lines as he replied. "The amount they feed us would starve the smallest mouse in the field, and you know it to be true. I merely went to another line. They've always leftovers. You should do the same, Edward. You're twice my size. If I'm hungry, what must you be?"

"Honest, lad. I be honest. They feed us what they feed us, and that is that." Then he tried a different approach to reach the boy. "And what am I to tell your mum? That her son, the *thief*, was whipped to death?" Tommy lowered his eyes in sudden guilt. "I promised to take care of ye, boyo. Is this how ye repay me?"

"No, Uncle." Tommy looked down at the unopened pail. He knew if he ignored his uncle and ate the beans, they would burn all the way down. He offered the tin to Edward.

"You eat it then, Edward. You haven't been looking too healthy since the boss took the lash to you."

Edward's eyebrows lowered and his eyes darkened. His voice reduced to an ominous rumble. "When I be feeble enough to be needing your charity, lad, I'll let you know." Tommy could almost hear lightning break around the edges of the words. Edward's eyes flashed at the perceived insult. Tommy hadn't intended the words to be an affront. He didn't want to provoke his uncle. Edward had been a prize fighter in his youth. His scarred face and flattened nose told tales of battles Tommy couldn't imagine. The spoon in the older man's hand was dwarfed by the immense fist. Tommy never wished to be on the receiving end of that fist.

"Now if you wish to make proper use of that food, why don't you take it to old Angus, the Scot. He needs to heal that bad leg, and can use the extra ration."

Tommy nodded his head, and slid off the stone onto the broken ground. "This will be the last we will discuss this, Tommy. Do ye understand?" The words were clear as a bell to Tommy. The theft would never be mentioned again, and he had better not ever *do* it again.

As Tommy moved off with his ill-gotten gain, Edward shook his head sadly. The boy had his mother's mischievous spirit, to be sure. Edward hoped he could curb the fire in Tommy's soul before the management did it for him. They wouldn't be so gentle as to merely scold.

The wind picked up just then and the sharp clang of the metal spoon twirling around the metal triangle warned Edward the meal break was over. He wiped the last bits of sauce from his rough beard with the edge of a sleeve. Then he delivered the dented tin into the basket on the walkway of the rail car and returned to where his sledgehammer lay. The wind began to howl. Thick snowflakes swirled around him. As the cloth covering his wounded back moistened, the open flesh began to sting. Edward ignored the pain, as he always did, and picked up his hammer. The sound of metal on rock filled his ears, over the whistling wind. Slowly, he began his task of breaking the huge stone boulders into small pieces that could be hauled away in wheelbarrows. The stone yielded to the hammer, urged on by his muscle. Blasting the rocks would be easier, but he'd been told pyrotechnics were too expensive to be wasted on *their* kind. At least with the wind, the dust wasn't so bad. Some days, Edward coughed constantly. The mucus was tinted grey when it exited his throat.

Edward turned his body so he could look east. Mile upon mile of rail gleamed behind them. He knew the hardest task was upon them. Mickey O'Toole had said it couldn't be done. No man would ever run rails through this cañon. Even if they could, he'd wanted no part of it. No matter what the money, he couldn't stand the brutality any more, he claimed. Mickey had disappeared in the night, determined to find his fortune in the silver fields of Aspen. Edward wished him well.

Edward didn't know what lay ahead, but it didn't matter. He would see this road completed. The money was important to him. And today was payday.

He swung the hammer until it struck the steel chisel again, then watched the big rock finally split. The two pieces hovered for a moment. Finally, half fell into the river with a crash. His back hurt, so he thought instead of Maggie. Thought of her shining hair, and her blue eyes, the color of a summer sky. Soon he would have money enough to bring her here, to this land where they could make a home. The next time his hammer struck, he was smiling.

# CHAPTER 7

Luke was engrossed in the blueprints of the road route when the sudden slowing of the engine made him raise his head. They were nowhere near the new construction. They had just left the Red Cliff station, where they had stopped briefly to fill the boiler. Luke loosely rolled the prints and stacked them against the wall of the car. The other men ignored him. Once the train was almost stopped, he went to the door and stepped out into the storm. It was snowing hard here in the mountains and it took him a moment to get his bearings. He spotted Jarrod Talbot speaking low and earnestly with one of the engineers. Luke remembered his name was George Moore.

"Is there a problem?" Luke asked as he joined the two men. The wind was blowing directly in his face, and it took his breath away. He tilted his head down so he could breathe easier. He could only glance up into the other man's face from time to time. The blowing snow stung his eyes.

"Don't rightly know yet," George said. He was having the same problem with speaking. "There's a slide up ahead. Glen's gone to see if we can break through it, or if we're going to have to go back to Leadville to get a snow breaker."

Luke nodded. He could see the pile of snow that covered the tracks and blocked their path. Avalanches were common in the spring, as the heavy, wet snow packed on top of older, finer snow. Sometimes an engine could break through a small slide. If the pile of snow on the tracks was too large, only the brute force of a specially made engine would clear the road. Sometimes even that was not enough. Then the only option would be to tunnel through the slide, making a temporary passage until the snow melted.

A figure appeared through the swirling snow to Luke's right.

"Well?" Jarrod asked in a loud voice. It was hard to hear over the sound of the wind in the trees.

Glen Fay's large face was red from the wind and the cold. Small icicles had formed on his rough black moustache. They cracked and fell to the ground when he spoke. "It's pretty big, but I think if we can dig in about three feet, the engine can take it. We've got the tools, and we've got the men. I think it's time for them to earn their keep."

Luke agreed. The men were already being paid for their journey. They would simply have to start working a little sooner. Jarrod looked to Luke for guidance. "Me and my men will still have to guard the gold. We can't help. You up to starting your job early?"

Luke nodded. "I'll roust 'em up. George, if you and Glen could open up the tool car and start unloading shovels, we'll be out of here in no time flat." The men moved quickly to their assignments.

Luke appeared in the lead car, and announced, "Okay, men! Report to the tool car. We've got a slide to clear, or we'll be spending the night up here."

Most of the men stood and began to button heavy coats and slip on thick gloves. But several of the men grumbled and remained where they were.

Luke didn't wait idly. He strode down the aisle, moving men aside. He stood before the first of the men, a slender man in his twenties, and asked, in a voice meant to carry, "Do you have a problem, Mister?" It was only through conscious effort he said 'mister' instead of 'soldier'.

"Be reasonable!" the man replied. "Look at the weather. Why don't we go back and get a plow car?"

The rest of the men waited, wondering what the reply would be. Luke nodded slowly, lips pursed as though thinking. He was thinking all right, but not about going back for help. "The way I see it," Luke said sternly, "You've got a choice. You can either get your tail in gear and help us get to the job, or you can sit here where it's nice and warm. And you'll stay nice and warm because you won't be getting off the train at the cañon. You'll be heading right back to Denver, 'cause we don't need slackers on this project." He paused, letting the threat sink in. "What'll it be?"

Two other men who had remained seated during the conversation stood and began donning their gear. The man facing Luke continued to sit, looking stubborn. "I didn't plan on having to work in the snow."

One of the other men who was ready to exit the car spoke. "We're going to the mountains, boy! It's still winter in the high country. There's snow where we're going, too!" Snow blew in when he pulled open the car door. Then he left the car. Other men started to follow. They had chosen their path. Luke waited for the man he faced to choose his.

He remained seated, looking stubborn. "I didn't plan on no snow! It's nearly summer, dadblame it!"

"What's your name?" asked Luke.

"Eli Moss," replied the man in a sullen voice.

Luke nodded. He turned to see Jarrod entering the car. The three men were the only ones remaining.

"Is there a problem here?" asked Jarrod.

"There's no problem at all," Luke replied, as he buttoned the top of his coat, and pulled his hat down lower on his face. "Jarrod, Mr. Eli Moss here has decided he doesn't wish to work with us. So he's no longer employed by the road. Make sure he either gets off the train at the cañon, or collect a fare from him for the return trip."

Eli looked startled, as Jarrod took a long look at him, memorizing his face. "I'll make sure, Luke."

Luke walked halfway down the car and turned to face Moss one more time. "If you decide to join us outside, find me. We'll talk about your continued employment."

As he opened the car door, the wind took his breath away once more. Over the wind in his ears, he heard Moss ask Jarrod, "Who is that man?"

Luke didn't hear Jarrod's response. He was already outside. Fine, if the secret was out, so be it.

With fifty-plus men shoveling, it didn't take long to clear three feet. The wind, snow, and cold made the effort difficult, but the workers kept their backs to their task. Glen frequently walked the slide to check on progress. He reported to Luke. The other men realized quickly who was in charge, and began to report to him without asking. Eli Moss never appeared outside. It wasn't really a surprise, but he had hoped for better from the man. He had been around other men who didn't want to work in life, but he couldn't really understand the notion.

When Glen reported, not quite an hour later, that the engine could break through, Luke stopped the men. They loaded the shovels back in the tool car and took their places again in the passenger cars. Eli Moss still sat in the same place. Those who looked at him either glared, or shook their heads angrily, muttering things under their breath. The rest simply ignored him. Three of the plush velvet seats now held three men because nobody wished to sit beside or across from Moss.

Luke shook his head too. He wasn't angry. He was sad. Some people simply would never know the joy of a job well done. Still, it was Eli's loss, and his lesson to learn.

The engine slowly reversed course. It needed to attain a certain speed before it reached the slide to break through. If the engineer calculated wrong, the men would be back outside soon. This time, to dig out the engine. Luke didn't think the slide was wide enough to derail the train, although that had occurred in the past, as well. If that happened, they *would* be spending the night on the mountain while someone, probably Luke or Jarrod, rode one of the mules they carried, back to the Leadville depot for help. Red Cliff was only a way station. They didn't have the proper equipment to re-rail a train.

When the engine had backed several miles, it stopped. Luke felt a thrumming underfoot as the crew stoked the fire, building pressure. When the engineer opened up the throttle Luke was nearly thrown out of his seat by the force. He pushed himself back and held on to one of the support poles. He watched thick, black smoke mingle with the driving snow. It rushed by the windows in a charcoal-gray haze as the train built speed. Other men in the car braced hands on other supports or the edges of their seats to help lessen the impact when the engine struck the snowbank. If the engine couldn't break the drift, the men would be tossed around the cars and likely end up injured.

Faster and faster the train moved. The cars swayed on the tracks in the wind. Luke could feel his heart beating almost as fast as the engine vibration underfoot. The engine didn't sound a whistle, since that could bring down another avalanche. Even the racing engine was a danger, but a necessary one. Luke had estimated the approximate distance to the drift in his head but the impact still came as a surprise. There was a sudden lurch and shudder as the front of the engine buried into the drift. The cars actually bounced up off the rails for an instant. There was a hesitation as the engine pushed the huge pile of snow. Then, just as suddenly, a release came as it broke through. The men moved away from the windows of the car as the pile of snow scraped down the sides of the cars as they passed. One window near the back of the car cracked from the pressure as the train shot through the opening.

The locomotive slowed and then stopped on the tracks a little further up the way, so the crew could assess the damage to the train. Luke stepped out of the car to the cheers of the workers. They had made it through, and no one had been hurt! At least, thought Luke, in this car.

After he checked the other two passenger cars for injuries — there were none — Luke stepped out again into the storm and hurried toward the front of the train. Jarrod came up behind him fast, and then passed him by.

"Everything okay?" Luke asked as he neared the engine crew.

"Nothing that can't be fixed," George replied. "We bent up the cow catcher a bit, and I've got a cab full of snow. One of the windows busted out when we hit. But that won't cause us no trouble. Snow'll melt right fast."

Glen called out from underneath the engine. "It doesn't look like we bent anything up real bad," he said. "I think we can go on." He crawled out from under the huge, steaming engine carrying an oil wick torch. One advantage of a torch over a lantern was it wouldn't blow out, no matter how strong the wind. "Whew!" he exclaimed with a broad grin. "I wasn't real sure we'd make it through that. It was touch and go for a moment."

The men broke up, and Luke started back toward the passenger car. Jarrod caught up to him and yelled over the wind, "Why don't you sit back in the pay car with me? I can bring you up to date on the job."

Luke stopped for a moment, considering. Jarrod continued. "Might as well. The men have already figured out you're some sort of foreman."

"You're probably right," Luke replied.

"We've got coffee in the back . . . The real stuff. Not chicory," tempted Jarrod with a smile.

Luke laughed. He ended the laugh with a cough, as the wind changed direction suddenly.

Jarrod knocked once on the door to the gold car, and then again, three times quickly. A face Luke recognized vaguely from Denver appeared at the window. His eyes quickly lost a suspicious look when he saw Jarrod and Luke, and he hurried to open the door.

"About time!" Jarrod said, stomping his feet at the door's entrance. "It's blasted *cold* out there!"

"I suppose you'd rather I just open the door when anyone knocks?" asked the tall, slim man with the heavy moustache.

Jarrod didn't respond to the thinly veiled sarcasm. Instead, he walked to the other end of the room, which was about half the length of the car, and picked up a large, china coffee mug with a steam engine painted on the side.

"Nice mug," commented Luke.

"Got it for my tenth service year," Jarrod replied proudly. He held it up so Luke could see the wide gold-leaf lettering that read, "J.E. Talbot." Underneath his name was the familiar "D.&R.G.R.W."

After pouring two cups of steaming coffee, Jarrod and Luke sat down on facing velvet-covered wing chairs that seemed to be bolted to the floor.

"They are bolted," Jarrod replied to the question in Luke's eyes. "The boys and I spend a lot of time in this car, goin' back and forth along the line. We wanted to be comfortable, so this was the compromise. We can't move them, but they're nice and soft. Looks just like a parlor in some fancy house, huh?"

Luke had to agree. The floor had a rug from the Orient, and there were tables and lamps in a design that *did* look like a parlor. Luke settled back into the green velvet and asked, "What can you tell me about the job?"

Jarrod took several sips of his coffee before he responded. "You're walking into a tough post."

Luke smiled. "I'd hardly expect anything different. It's a tight schedule and a lot of men."

Jarrod shook his head. "You don't understand. That's normal. But there's lots of politics right now."

"Such as?"

"Too many chiefs and not enough injuns," remarked the man who let them in the door. "That's the problem. Ricker's got everyone at each other's throats."

Luke's eyes narrowed. "*Colonel* Ricker?" he asked. "The roadmaster from Leadville?"

Jarrod shook his head. "Not no more. Now, he's *General Superintendent* Ricker. You'll be reporting to him."

"I was told I am supposed to report directly to Mr. Jackson," Luke replied carefully. He should have known there would be a hierarchy of command!

The five men in the car exchanged glances, even stopping a game of poker to look at Jarrod.

"Well . . .," Jarrod replied. "That may be. There's no love lost between Jackson and Ricker. But Jackson's leaving. No telling who's replacing him. If it's Moffat . . . well, Ricker's like the son he never had. Any enemy of Palmer's is a friend of his."

Luke took in that information. No wonder Moffat was less than friendly, considering Palmer had recommended him. "Even so," Luke commented, "They need this road built. Surely, they won't stand in the way."

One of the men at the table let out a short bark of a laugh.

"No," Jarrod agreed. "Everyone wants the road built. But only if it doesn't affect all the little kingdoms that have been built up since the General left. When Palmer was the president, everybody knew who the boss was. After he left, and David Dodge was fired, well, it sort of left who was in charge up in the air."

"You bet!" said the door guard. "Chapman thinks *he's* the boss."

"And John Connell thinks *he's* the boss," supplied one of the poker players.

"And who are *they*?" Luke asked.

"Okay," Jarrod replied. "Let me give you the rundown. Ricker is the general super. He stays in Denver, and'll pretty much keep out of your hair. J.R. Chapman is the superintendent of bridges, which covers new construction. But all orders to him have to go through the assistant superintendent, which is Quimby Lamplugh, in Leadville."

The door guard joined in the conversation. "Quimby's okay, but John Connell, the assistant roadmaster in Leadville, will make you tear your hair out. He has full control of material shipment, so you'll have to tread real light-like."

Jarrod continued. "Plus, Glenwood Springs is a new area. Word came down that the section foreman in Gypsum is gonna be a new roadmaster for the Gypsum to Glenwood stretch, so Ricker's got a real bee in his bonnet right now."

Jarrod nodded. "And Carpenter's no prize, neither. He and Connell are buddies. Even though it ain't your fault Carpenter's out, you're hand picked by Palmer. Word of that will get out like wildfire. The workers will be pleased to see you come on, but it won't win you no friends in management."

By this time, Luke had set his mug gently on the nearest table and was rubbing the top of his nose bridge with his thumb and index fingers. "I see what you mean," he commented without looking at Jarrod.

"'Least you can still back out," said the door guard. "The rest of us are stuck with it. I could go to another company, but I've got seniority now. A pension. I don't dare leave."

"Anything else I need to know?" Luke asked.

"I know there are a lot of problems with the men in the cañon right now. Don't know much about the situation but word has it supplies are tight. And you know what they say about idle hands," Jarrod said.

Luke shook his head with sad amusement. "I thought when the Baby Road started building again it might get better on that front. Nothing's changed at all, huh?"

"Sure it has," Jarrod remarked. "Things are *much* worse."

# CHAPTER 8

Luke spent a pleasant hour learning about the personalities of some of the men he would have to deal with day-to-day. Jarrod promised to introduce Luke to the foreman of the track materials yard in Gypsum. "You'll need to be on good terms with him. He's got the whole line — where everything is and how to get it — right in his head."

"A good man to know," Luke agreed.

"I don't know how many of the foremen you'll be keeping on after you get there," Jarrod said, "But I can tell you, you'll want to get rid of at least three. Alex Sneed, on the Rock Gang, the head of the Blasting Crew, and the crew chief of Water Service. They're all hand picked by Carpenter, and if you don't get rid of them . . . ." He left the thought uncompleted.

Luke picked up and finished the sentence, "They'll somehow get rid of me."

"Bright boy," commented Danial to Jarrod. "I think he'll do."

Luke chuckled at the compliment. He was about to ask another question when the train began to slow.

"We must be getting near Gypsum," Jarrod commented. "We'd best get started." The other men seated around a small table in the corner laid down their cards and stood.

"Anything I can do?" Luke asked, understanding the pay crew would start getting payroll ready for the workers at the Gypsum station.

"You'll need to leave," Jarrod said. "I'm a man shy, but the rules are real clear. Ya mind?"

Luke wasn't insulted. He wasn't a paymaster and the rules *were* clear. He donned his coat and hat, said his good-byes, and exited the front of the pay car. The train was still moving, so he held carefully onto the handrail and stepped lightly across the coupler to the next car. He saw movement on top of the car and raised his head to see Glen scampering across the top of the cars, setting the hand brakes on each. He moved with the grace of a squirrel, hopping from car to car, the wind and snow seeming to have no effect on him.

He nodded to Luke as he hopped over him. Luke watched for a moment as Glen spun the wheel that would clamp down steel brakes to slow the wheels of each car. Without setting the brakes on each individual car, the brakes on the engine would burn out, trying to slow down the entire train. A runaway train with no track at the end of the line would not be a pretty sight. After Glen finished with the pay car, he moved to the mail service car.

The wind was biting, so Luke turned and opened the door of the elegant wood and velvet passenger car. General Palmer had spared no expense in having the finest passenger cars built. They had fountains to drink from, and privies at each end. The overstuffed velvet seats were surrounded by polished brass and oiled oak. It was nice to ride in style for once. Luke knew once he arrived in the cañon, boxcars and tight quarters would be the order of the day. One of the men was exiting the privy as Luke entered the door. There was a quick shuffle while they passed.

Luke settled back into the seat he had vacated when the train stopped for the slide. The men had left it for him. It was only a few minutes before they reached the Gypsum station. Luke took the opportunity to go forward and speak to George and Glen, and compliment them on handling the slide. He watched as they filled the boiler with fresh water and re-stocked the coal tinder. Luke wanted to get a look at the camp as they arrived, and Glen agreed to give up his seat for the last few minutes of the journey. The train took on two more cars of coal for the construction front. Sack upon sack of grain was loaded into a partly empty car.

When the train was ready to depart, Glen walked its length to take a seat in the caboose. Luke sat on the right side of the huge engine and had a clear view of the surrounding scenery. The high, craggy mountains gave way abruptly to lush valley. Trees, newly budding, and the beginnings of green grass moved past the train so quickly that Luke's eyes couldn't focus on any single item. Snow dusted the ground and trees, although not as heavily as in the mountains. Talk was impossible over the booming of the massive engine between Luke and George, so they didn't try. Luke simply enjoyed the scenery and waited to reach the cañon with rising anticipation.

When the train rounded a bend twenty or so minutes later, Luke caught the first glimpse of the base camp. Row upon row of green canvas tents dotted the landscape. They reminded Luke abruptly of Sherman's camp. Corrals had been built at the edge of the camp for the pack mules and other draft animals. A work train blew smoke, ready for a trip into the cañon. A rail-mounted crane loaded fresh steel onto a flatcar, and hundreds of men milled around. Luke was in awe of the extent of the camp. He felt his gut tighten with nerves. He may have bitten off more than he could chew.

Luke turned his head when he thought he heard George yelling over the sound of the engine. He couldn't hear, so he stood and walked around to the other side of the car. He bent down so his head was right next to George's. "What?" he yelled.

"I said, 'pretty impressive, huh?'" shouted George.

Luke smiled and nodded in response. He stood silently and watched as the train slowly entered the camp. George stopped the train to give the work engine room to move onto the Y-turn so it would be in a position to go directly into the cañon when the pay train passed by.

The sky was still overcast. The cañon walls disappeared into the mist, giving the impression of never-ending height. Jackson's description hadn't done it justice. The sheer magnitude of the cañon was nearly overwhelming. He felt very small and insignificant as he stared at the vast beauty of it. Although it was still early in the day, the sun was beginning to settle behind the mountain, lending an orange and pink haze to the mist. For a moment, the edge of the sun was visible. The sudden burst of sunlight danced off the snow that delicately dusted the rocks and trees. It made them sparkle like diamonds. Then it slowly dipped its head behind the granite peak for the night.

A strange feeling came over Luke. He had never stood in this spot, but felt as though he had. He was home. There was no other word for it. Somehow, something deep inside him recognized this place, felt a part of the rocks and trees and rushing water. He knew what lay around the next bend. The sensation resonated inside him, swirled over his skin like the touch of a mother's hand — warm, safe. He was, in that second, at peace with the craggy granite jutting up from the earth. He knew it. Understood it.

This place had always been and would always be. The men assembled might be able to bend the cañon to their will, might be able to lay tracks through her, but this place would be, long after they were dead, long after the tracks they laid were dissolved to rust. The cañon called to some part of Luke's insides, asked him to stay. It wanted someone that would respect the beauty and add to it, not destroy it. Luke's heart answered "yes" before he even fully recognized the question.

A jolt brought him back to his senses. The sensation dimmed to a dream. The work engine was fully on the side spur, and George had opened the throttle slightly and sounded the whistle to let the men know he was coming forward. When the train had moved into the place occupied by the work train moments before, George throttled down and braked to a stop. A man in a wet wool jacket strode up to the engine as George and Luke descended the stairs.

"You're running late!" he yelled over the sound of the work engine, which was beginning to stoke up. "We expected you here hours ago!"

George raised his voice in return. "Ran into a slide on top of the hill. Had to dig it out." The other man nodded, and then glanced at Luke, who was just swinging down from the black steel ladder.

"Glen not working today?" asked the man of George.

George gestured with a thumb. "He's back in the caboose. This here's Luke Ballister, the new . . . " He paused for a split second, then continued, "surveyor foreman, out of Denver. He'll only be staying a few days. Could you do me a favor and introduce him to the survey crew chief?" George turned to Luke and explained. "Amos here will take you to the surveyor who's been heading up the crew since Chuck got killed last month." George gave a mock salute and walked away from the other two men.

Amos gestured for Luke to follow him. When they were a sufficient distance from the engine, they could speak. "That's better," Amos said when they could hear each other again. "I swear I'll be totally deaf by the time I retire," he said with a shake of his head. He stuck a finger in his left ear and moved it back and forth vigorously. "Blasted ears are still ringing."

Luke nodded and turned to watch the various areas of activity, from unloading the boxcars on the newly-arrived train, to Jarrod's men beginning to set up their materials to issue pay. What struck Luke most was that with all the activity, there seemed to be no order. A foreman to his left shouted a command to a group of workmen, only to have someone else appear moments later and direct the same men to a different task.

Amos was looking left and right, trying to find the person George had asked him to locate. "I don't see him nowhere," Amos said. "You wait here. I'll send him to you," he remarked and quickly moved off.

Luke was pleased to be left alone for a few minutes. He wanted to watch things more carefully. Fortunately, with the arrival of the pay train Jarrod and his men were the focus of attention. Luke was left undisturbed. He sat down on a large boulder. A friendly dog nudged his arm with an eager nose and Luke reached down to scratch behind the ears of the hound. A thumping sound made Luke look down. The dog's leg moved rhythmically in time to Luke's ministrations. Luke smiled and scratched harder. The dog sighed contentedly, closed its eyes, and rested its muzzle on Luke's leg.

Luke watched brief exchanges at each car. An argument seemed to be going on in front of the boxcar where he had watched the grain being loaded. They couldn't have unloaded it that quickly! Where was the grain?

Curiosity got the better of him. He moved the dog's head, and stood. The hound, unperturbed, laid down beside the rock and rested its nose on its paws.

Luke moved close enough he could hear the exchange of voices.

"I tell you, we brought twenty bags of grain!" Glen was saying, his voice indignant.

"Well, they're not here!" replied the roughshod man. "And even if they was, twenty bags would only feed a quarter of the stock! What's wrong with you people? What do we have to do to get supplies?!? My animals are going to starve in this hellhole."

Luke watched Glen's jaw set angrily. "I only run the engine, Clarence. I don't know anything about what you ordered. You'll have to take it up with Gypsum. That's where they were loaded. And I have no idea where the twenty bags went. We didn't stop once from the time we left Gypsum."

"That's not quite true," Luke replied almost unconsciously, forgetting himself.

Both men turned abruptly. "What did you say?" Clarence asked.

"Luke," Glen said, "I didn't see you standing there." Then his face brightened. "But, hey, you saw them load the grain too, didn't you? Tell Clarence we had the supplies he asked for."

Luke nodded briefly. "I watched them load grain. I don't know how much for certain, but they loaded at least ten bags before I left. But what I was saying was that we did stop the train. When the work engine was turning. We sat there for at least ten minutes." Luke mused, almost to himself, "I was up front, so I couldn't hear or see much, and I can't imagine who would take the grain, or how many men it would take to move that many bags in so short a time."

Clarence, somewhat mollified by Luke's agreement, nodded his head slowly. "It's not the first time. Weird stuff's been going on. I think we got us some two-legged varmints hereabouts." Then he shook his head and started to move off. "I'm going to see if I can get someone to telegraph for more grain, and report the theft. Don't know what I'm going to do about the stock. Ain't nothing for them to eat for miles."

Glen looked at Luke with thanks. "Appreciate the assist, Luke. I'll let George know what happened." Then he left too.

Luke returned to his rock, thinking. Was it just nearby ranchers, taking the grain for their own stock, or something more serious?

The sudden, bright sound of rattling chains made him look up.

A boxcar near the end of the train was being unloaded. Luke was surprised to see the car held ten men, bound with chains at both wrist and ankle. Two men stood on each side of the group, armed with rifles. So, the road had hired a contractor to pick up hitchers. Luke was a little surprised, but it certainly wasn't uncommon. The men would work as convict labor until they paid for their fare to the cañon, plus the cost of any supplies they had absconded with when they left. After those items had been paid, they would be free to continue to work for the road, or leave as they saw fit. No hard feelings. It was just business. Still, the contractors were seldom gentle in their persuasions, since they were paid per man caught.

A whistle blast made Luke glance into the cañon. The work train was returning with a crew of men. The job would be shutting down early today, as it did each payday. On any other job, Luke knew the men would hightail it into the nearest town to gamble or buy female companionship. Luke wasn't sure whether anyone could get to town and back in a single night on this job.

The work train backed out of the cañon and stopped just inches from the front of the pay train. Steam engines are built to go either forward or backward so it was easier to simply run the train in reverse rather than build extra track to turn it around. The engine controls were positioned so that the engineer could face either direction and use them effectively.

Amos had completely disappeared and Luke didn't want to accidentally miss the surveyor foreman so he remained seated on the boulder, the blue-point hound at his side, and watched the line form in front of the pay car.

One man was head and shoulders above the rest — as broad across as two lesser men. He had thick, dark red hair, loosely tied with a strip of rawhide. He kept glancing around as he moved toward the head of the line. The closer he got, the more agitated he became. He was obviously looking for someone and couldn't find him. No surprise, considering the hundreds of men milling about. As each man reached the table where Jarrod sat, he would recite his name and Jarrod would search a record, then make a mark by the name. Afterward, the man would sign or, if he couldn't write, put his mark on the paper. Once each of these steps was accomplished, the man would receive a stack of coin money. The men were generally paid once per month, although Luke had worked some jobs where it was more frequent.

A separate table and line near the tents was nearly a twin to the one directly in front of Luke. That line contained only Chinese workers, and the paymaster was also Chinese. The Celestials always appeared so . . . serene to Luke. Each man, after receiving his pay, would bow low, a sign of respect to the paymaster, then quietly step away. But Luke knew the Chinese had tempers, and that they could fight in a style that would put the best fisticuffs prize fighter flat in the dirt.

Already, men who had received their pay were setting up make-shift card games on flat boulders, or on tables near the kitchen car. Other men appeared to be tossing dice into a crudely-made pit, or against the edge of a rock. Shouts of delight and violent oaths would accompany each toss of the cubes of ivory. Luke knew that tonight some men would drink too much. Others would pick fights that had brewed over the previous month. Each month was a gamble to the rail-road how many men would disappear into the night with tools and supplies, hoping to make their fortune in the silver fields of Aspen.

Luke sensed, rather than heard, a commotion to his right, near the end of the pay train. Years of command experience warned him. It was not a good sound. He couldn't see the cause of the ruckus, but others had started to notice the noise. Most of the men in the pay line ignored the commotion until a man with curly, carrot-orange hair and freckles across a thin face suddenly approached, nearly running. He went directly to the big man, now at the front of the line. Luke couldn't hear the words spoken, but the effect was immediate. The tall man's face went from smiling at the first approach of the man, to concerned, to absolute fury. He broke away from the line, and headed toward the commotion, the smaller man at his heels. He pushed other men aside with impatience.

Luke followed. He had an eerie sense of foreboding.

# CHAPTER 9

Edward was getting nervous. Tommy was usually the first in line for pay. If he arrived before Edward received his pay, he would wait for him beside the table, where he was not considered a threat by the armed guards. Then, they would go together to the mail service car. Edward was ashamed to admit he could not read or write the English language. He could read his own native Gaelic, but he could not send his pay to his wife using that language. Tommy also sent money to his family, to better their lives. Since they lived in the same village, they would send one envelope to Ireland. Edward had learned the men in the mail service car were above reproach. They had no ties to the railroad. They worked for the government of the United States and would faithfully deliver the money without theft. He had checked. He had learned from his family by return mail that all of the money he had sent over the past year had arrived within only a month or two.

Tommy still hadn't appeared by the time Edward reached the front of the line. The older man was tall enough that he could see over the heads of most of the men, and although he saw shock after shock of red hair, none were attached to his nephew.

The man in front of Edward moved away. Suddenly, he was next next. The paymaster, Mr. Talbot, asked his name. He was about to reply when he heard a shout to his right.

"Edward!!" he heard, and turned to look, expecting to see Tommy. It wasn't Tommy. It was Pat Coughlin, a friend from a neighboring village in Ireland. Edward had helped Pat get his job with the road.

He beamed a smile at his friend, whom he hadn't seen in over a week.

Pat didn't return the smile. He looked nearly frantic. "Edward, you've got to come! They've got Tommy! It's Sneed and the others!"

"What do you mean, 'they've got him?'" Edward asked with growing concern.

"It's bad, Edward. They say he was stealing. They're beating him bloody." Pat grabbed Edward's arm, but couldn't get a hand around the huge bicep. "Please, Edward! It may already be too late!"

Fear replaced concern in Edward's eyes. Then he heard the commotion of voices. The fear quickly became anger. They had no right to beat him! He was only a boy!

Hundreds of men milled around, but Edward hardly saw them. He moved through the crowd as though he were a steam engine. Men either stepped aside or were moved by force.

He didn't see the tall, blonde man following in his wake.

# CHAPTER 10

Luke pushed through the crowd to confront a scene that turned his stomach. Dozens of men had formed a circle around a flat patch of rust-red ground near the river. Four men held the crowd back with the threat of long rifles. Those who passed them would be shot.

One man stood in the barren circle, holding the wooden handle of an axe. The end was bloody. He had collar-length black hair, now matted with sweat. An evil glint in cold dark eyes showed internal rage.

"Get up!" he shouted at a still form on the ground. He kicked at the body with a booted foot. "Get up, ya thieving potato eater!"

The body on the ground was twisted wrong. Not in a natural position. But Luke couldn't believe, couldn't imagine the truth of what he saw. The young man's face was a mass of blood. His eyes were swollen shut from repeated blows. His hair was dark and wet.

He spotted a boy of no more than 15, struggling to see the spectacle through the mob. "I need you to do me a favor, lad," Luke said, placing a firm hand on the boy's shoulder.

The boy turned and looked up into Luke's eyes. "Yessir?" he asked, a little nervously.

"Find the paymaster. His name is Jarrod," Luke said hurriedly. "Tell him Luke needs him. Remember my name. *Luke* needs him. Tell him to bring as many men as he can spare. If anyone with a gun stops you, tell them Luke sent you. Bring him here. And hurry!" He released the shoulder of the stunned boy.

There was no discussion, no question. He turned without a word and bolted into the crowd, using the tall steam engine as a reference to get through the gathering.

Luke turned again, and headed toward the fracas. He hoped Jarrod would be there to back him up. If not, he might be ending his career, possibly his life. He had already seen the group of armed men streaming toward the scene. No shots had been fired — yet.

The tall redhead wasn't speaking. He stared in horrified silence as Luke pushed through the last of the men. The dozens of onlookers were strangely silent. Some faces were angry, some horrified. Luke had seen worse during battle, but he was always unnerved at the sight of such brutality.

Luke knew that the young man, hardly more than a child, was too injured to survive, but the man standing over him was still prodding, still shouting at him to get up, to take his punishment. He swore, and called the lad names. He hadn't yet realized the result of his actions. Luke couldn't just stand by. If he was shot, so be it. He moved forward. One of the guards stepped forward as well, rifle cross ways in his arms, blocking Luke's path. Luke looked at the man with an intensity that, after a few moments, forced the man to back down. He lowered his weapon and let the blonde man pass, not really understanding why he had done so.

As Luke approached the black-haired man, he reached out and violently took away the axe handle.

"What the blazes do you think you're doing?!?" the man asked, looking around him for the first time, and seeing the rage on the faces of the surrounding crew. "Do you have any idea who I am?"

"Don't rightly care," Luke replied calmly into the silent, chilled air. "But I do know you're not going to touch this boy again. If you try, I'll lay you out right next to him."

Fury erupted on the face of the other man. "Boys, take out this trash!" he exclaimed. The armed men turned to his call.

A new voice spoke from the left. Jarrod Talbot's voice. "The first one of you to raise a rifle will be shot." The voice was cold and sure.

When the guards turned, they found five new men, rifles tight to shoulders, ready to shoot. There was no way any one of them could get off a shot before they were killed. Self-preservation won over loyalty. One by one, weapons dropped to the ground. The guards backed away, leaving the instigator standing alone with Luke and the fallen boy.

Luke knelt beside the boy, afraid of what he would find. He reached under the boy's hair. There was a deep dent in the bone over the left temple. When Luke's hand came away it was covered with blood, and other, thicker matter. Although it was a useless effort, Luke felt the side of the boy's neck. He moved his fingers slowly, then finally placed his entire palm on the neck, searching for any pulse.

There was none. No surprise.

He closed his eyes and sighed, not wanting to reveal the truth. Not wanting to start a riot. Already people murmured in the background. Tension crackled in the air.

The dark-haired man still trembled with anger, his breathing was too fast, too shallow. Luke felt his own anger rising. He couldn't think of anything, short of rape or torture, that could raise a level of rage sufficient to beat a child to death. Whoever this man was, Luke wanted no part of him. He would be the first to go.

"So," Luke thought to himself, "*I've decided. No turning back now.*"

An older man, short and thickly built, abruptly pushed through the crowd, wheezing heavily. He carried a black doctor's bag. He tried to push past Luke to reach the fallen boy but Luke caught his eye and gave a small shake of his head. Doctors are for the living. He wasn't needed.

Riley Skelton preferred to be called "Skel." He saw the look that the blonde man gave him, but he wouldn't believe it, couldn't believe it. Tommy was a good boy. He hoped to be a doctor himself someday.

Skel knelt beside Luke and examined the body in the same manner Luke had. The collective group fell silent again as he worked. Not even a breath stirred the air. When Skel's shoulders slumped — when he admitted defeat with bowed head — the crowd started to murmur again in earnest.

Luke placed a gentle hand on the doctor's shoulder when he saw the older man's eyes close in sadness. Then the two men stood simultaneously. The doctor walked straight to the red-haired man and placed a hand on one massive forearm. He forced himself to look into the startled eyes of the big Irishman.

"I'm sorry, Edward," he said softly and then moved into the crowd.

Edward's green eyes began to burn. No, not Tommy! But the pain quickly turned to anger. His blood raced faster. Adrenaline stirred thick muscles and he turned his full rage toward Alexander Sneed with an animal snarl. He started forward, his eyes intent only on the figure in the center of the circle. He almost didn't notice when he was stopped cold by a hand on his chest.

"You've a right, I'll grant, if he was your kin," said the tall blonde stranger, "but I can't let you do it. Back down now or I'll have to lock you up."

"What in the hell is going on??!" exclaimed Charles Carpenter, bulling his way through the crowd.

"Your man Sneed just killed this boy," Jarrod said strongly. "Cold-blooded murder."

Carpenter pointed down at Tommy's inert form, "This the one who was stealing food?" he asked Sneed

"He was," replied Sneed, partly in fear, but with an equal level of arrogance. "He needed to be disciplined. Made an example of. Can't have people stealing from the road."

Luke spoke up. His words were ice cold. "You feeding these men so little that they're forced to steal?" The question started the murmuring again. Nobody seemed to know this man. Why was he standing up for them?

"That's none of your affair, mister," Carpenter replied. "I run this job, and I say that discipline keeps the crews running right."

"Discipline doesn't include murder," Luke replied, anger growing in his voice.

"I'll decide what discipline includes on my job. Alex had my permission to seek redress for the Denver & Rio Grande for its loss of supplies."

Luke gritted his teeth. He felt violated at the willful death of a boy he didn't know. The Denver & Rio Grande had no death wish against its employees. Luke couldn't believe that Jackson and Moffat would have any part of this decision. He had met other men like Carpenter. A leader in name, but only for his own glory, for his own gain. Carpenter believed he could not be held to task for his leadership decisions. That might be true in the bloody depths of war, but not in civilized society.

Jarrod opened his mouth to reply, but Luke held up a hand to stop him. "That might have been true in the past," he said quietly, "but no more. I'd rather have handled this differently, more politely, but the choices you and yours have made forced my hand. Pack your things and go, Carpenter." He pointed at Sneed, "This man will be held over for the sheriff — if there is one in Glenwood Springs — to stand trial for murder."

Hundreds of men held a collective breath, watching the exchange. The blonde had the armed pay crew at his back, but Carpenter had more men, vicious men with little sense of fair play.

Carpenter's reply was angry. "Whoever you are, I won't be spoken to that way. I am a former lieutenant in the Fourth New York Calvary, and the gang boss of this project." His voice raised to a controlled yell. Veins bulged in his neck, and he took a step toward Luke.

Luke held his ground and his temper. He reached an expectant hand backward, and Jarrod placed the two sealed envelopes into it.

"And I say, you will be spoken to that way," Luke replied, his voice flat. "If we're going to bring rank into this, I am a retired colonel in the New England Seventh Artillery, third in command under General Sherman, and the *new* gang boss of this project."

Luke broke the red wax seal on the first envelope and read the contents out loud.

"To Whom it May Concern: Please be advised that the bearer of this letter, Colonel Luke Ballister, has been retained by the Denver & Rio Grande Railroad in the position of gang boss of the Red Cliff to Aspen Spur. Please provide your cooperation toward this end. Signed, William Jackson, President, D&RGRR."

Luke stepped forward and held the second sealed envelope out toward Carpenter. Carpenter's eyes were still dark with anger, but also wide with surprise. "This envelope contains your instructions to return to Denver for reassignment. I thought you might prefer to read it in private."

Carpenter never reached out for the envelope. Luke held it out for a time, then dropped it at his feet.

"Your choice," Luke said with a shrug. "But you are leaving." As he turned and walked away, he heard a sharp click. It was an unmistakable sound. He turned slowly, not reaching for his sidearm. Carpenter held a Colt .45 steadily on him. Luke didn't speak a word. He wasn't sure what would set the man off.

"You need to drop the gun, Charlie," Jarrod said softly. "You don't have many friends in this group right now. You'd be dead before the bullet left the barrel."

Carpenter was shaking now. His eyes narrowed, his lips were tight and bloodless. "You won't take this from me!" he exclaimed with deadly intent.

"I think it's about time that *all* of you dropped your weapons!" The authoritative bass came from Luke's right, but he didn't take his eyes off Carpenter to see who it was.

The crowd parted to reveal a tall, thin man wearing a battered, gray Stetson. A silver star graced his cowhide vest. He held a double-barreled shotgun at hip level. It was pointed toward Luke and Carpenter.

"Deputy, what are you doing here?" Jarrod asked.

"Came to collect one of your prisoners. He broke up the saloon before your man grabbed him, and the owner pressed charges," the Deputy Sheriff replied. "I didn't realize I was coming into a war zone."

The moment when Carpenter glanced at the newcomer was all Luke needed. Quick as a flash, he drew his Colt Dragoon and held it steady. He doubted Carpenter had any more regard for the law than Sneed, and Luke didn't like being at a disadvantage. Carpenter looked back in surprise and alarm.

The Deputy let out an exasperated sigh and cocked the hammer on the first barrel. "I *thought* I said to drop 'em, not pick 'em up!"

"I will if he will," Luke replied quietly. "I don't have any quarrel with Mr. Carpenter, Deputy, but I won't be put down like a coyote after a calf."

Jarrod took the first step. He lowered his rifle and let it drop to the red dust. The other railroad men followed suit. Carpenter shook in earnest now, unsure of what to do.

"Come on now, Charlie, let's not make this more than it is," said the Deputy. "Just put up the gun, and you can go on your way."

Carpenter's breathing was fast and shallow. He glanced this way and that. Even with the pay crew having dropped their rifles, he was still outnumbered two to one. He didn't know much about the new man, but Gawdamighty, that was a fast draw! And he knew Deputy Martindale would blow a hole in him the size of the redhead's fist if he even flinched. Sweat dripped down his brow and stung his eyes. He blinked again and again, trying to decide what to do. The Deputy would let him go, would let him walk. He could get reassigned. He had done a good job. The road wouldn't let him go. Yeah, that was it. He just needed a new place. Nothing here to be killed over.

Carpenter's thumb moved toward the hammer, and both Luke and the Deputy waited with stilled breath. Luke felt that same odd calm fill him as he waited. He had killed before in defense, quickly and efficiently.

When Carpenter released the hammer on his Colt, Luke felt his heart beat again. It seemed like it had stopped for those few seconds.

Sneed had watched the confrontation with growing concern. Without Carpenter's backing, he was a goner. While all eyes followed the test of wills in front of him, Sneed slowly backed from the downed body of the red-headed thief, hoping to slip away in the confusion. He pushed his way into a small group of his loyal followers and they let him pass, hid his movements from the crowd. But one man saw.

Once past the crowd, Sneed made for the corral. He had just placed a saddle on a coal-black mule when a massive hand caught the back of his neck. The grip was tight enough, not only to make escape impossible, but to make him dizzy and lightheaded.

"Sneed!" came a vicious voice from behind him. "You'll be answering for my nephew now — may the Lord have mercy on his soul." A second hand spun him around, the hand on his neck loosening just enough to allow the movement. Then it tightened again until he was gasping for air. He looked up — and up — to stare into the enraged face of the boy's uncle, Edward O'Malley.

"You shouldn't ought to have harmed the boy," Edward said with deadly calm. "I could take your abuse, Sneed, your lashes, but Tommy . . .," he said, faltering as he thought about the sight of the still body. Alex Sneed watched those tear-filled green eyes harden into emerald stone.

Edward clenched his hand into a fist and cocked back his enormous arm. One strike of his fist had killed an opponent in the ring, shattering his face and lodging the bones of his jaw in his brain. That was when he had left boxing. But this . . . this was personal and he felt no guilt.

Sneed, panic-stricken, twisted and turned in Edward's grasp. He clawed at the enormous fist, fighting to break free. But there was no relief from the ever-tightening grip.

"You'll have to let him go, son," said a booming bass to Edward's right. "This is a matter for the law."

Edward turned flashing eyes toward the Deputy, but he didn't release Sneed. Nor lower his arm. "I pledged an oath to protect Tommy, Constable. I failed him. I failed his mum. But I *will* avenge him. It's me sworn duty!"

Luke moved toward Edward, standing between the Deputy's gun and the Irishman's anger. "You'll best avenge your kin by doing as the Deputy says," Luke said reasonably, hoping his plan would succeed. Luke had just learned from Carpenter that the boy was the big man's nephew. Edward's words had confirmed it.

"It'll be hard enough for your sister to have lost her boy," Luke said. "Do you think she wants to lose you both? Who'll support her?" Luke watched as his words shook the big man. His arm faltered, his eyes showed confusion.

The lawman watched the effect of Luke's words on Edward, as his eyes closed and a single tear traced silver down his cheek.

"The Colonel's right," said Deputy Martindale, "We have laws in this country so the common man can have justice without endangering himself." The Deputy holstered his gun and walked carefully toward the pair.

Edward's eyes grew cold again. "Justice? There is no justice for the Irish in this country, Constable! And 'tis no use to tell me other."

Sneed was almost limp in Edward's grasp from lack of air. Edward held his weight with no effort.

"I can't speak for other places," Martindale said, "But here in Colorado, the law stands for all men."

Edward watched the Constable's face. He truly believed the words he spoke. He glared at Sneed for a moment, then jumped as Martindale placed a tentative hand on his arm. He locked eyes with the Deputy for long moments.

Finally, Edward dropped Sneed from his grasp with a disgusted look and backed away. Sneed coughed repeatedly, filling his starving lungs with air.

"Take him then, Constable!" Edward said with undisguised loathing. "Take this evil son of Satan and hang him until he meets his master. I'll not bloody my hands with the likes of him!"

# CHAPTER 11

By the time Luke and the others returned to the fallen boy, the body had been covered with a blanket. The man with the medical bag began to speak quietly with Edward, discussing whether to ship the body back to Ireland.

Luke's heart stopped again for a brief moment when the weighty boom of a shotgun echoed through the canyon. He and the others rushed toward the sound.

When Luke broke through the crowd, he saw the Deputy standing over the still form of Alexander Sneed. At Luke's questioning look, the Deputy explained. "Dang fool made a grab for my sidearm. I had no choice." Several men nodded agreement.

Martindale shook his head in annoyance. "Judge Hale won't be pleased. No, sir! 'A man is entitled to his day before his peers,' he always says. He'll be right angry with me."

"We can probably spare one of these men as a witness, if you have need," Luke said, looking to the men for a volunteer. Before he could say anything else, he heard a nearly forgotten, snide voice behind him.

"Well, well. Two men dead on the ground. It figures that you're nearby!" The biting sarcasm was evident. Luke turned to find Colonel Robert Ricker, sneering down at him from a light brown mule. "You know, Ballister, you're like some sort of black cloud. What idiot hired you?"

Luke replied calmly, "I'd be careful of the way you speak about the president of the road, if I were you." He was pleased at Ricker's openmouthed disbelief.

"President Moffat would *never* hire you, even to break rocks!" Ricker exclaimed. "He knows all about your sordid past down south!"

Luke's brow furrowed and his eyes narrowed. "First, *Jackson* is still president. But, yes, Moffat also offered me the post. As for the southern expansion, surely you're not going to try to accuse me of being responsible for the Royal Gorge Wars?"

"He'll blame anyone who was there," said a new, utterly disgusted voice. Luke turned his head to the words.

"You stay out of this, McMurtrie!" Ricker said, pointing a finger at the new man on a black mule. Luke found himself smiling as John

McMurtrie dismounted. He hadn't seen John in years — since they manned the barricade together outside of Cañon City.

"Glad to have you on board, Luke," said McMurtrie in greeting, "in whatever capacity. And if you're going to blame anyone for the mess down at the Gorge, Colonel Ricker," he continued in a low, harsh voice, "blame me. *I* was in charge. Even if nobody bothered to tell me it was urgent to arrive first, it was *my* decision to spend an extra night in La Veta."

"Your *decision* cost us the rail line through the Gorge," Ricker replied. "You and Ballister both! The Atchison Topeka should never have gotten a foothold there. As far as I'm concerned, Moffat was foolish to have anything to do with either of you!" Ricker wheeled his mount sharply and trotted toward the pay car.

"Good to see you John," Luke said with a small shake of his head. "I see that Colonel Ricker is still a ray of sunshine."

John McMurtrie sighed. "Don't antagonize him, Luke. We've got to work with him for the next six months. I've bitten my tongue to bleeding more times than I can count. I'm just trying to stay off his bad list. He's the one ordering supplies."

"Frankly, John," Luke said, "I'm surprised you'd hire back on with the D&RG. After President Lovejoy fired you and David Dodge — ." He left the statement hanging. The firing of General Palmer's key staff by his replacement was still a sore point with Luke.

John smiled, his thick mustache parting to reveal white teeth. "I consider Lovejoy's firing a badge of honor. And, no, I haven't hired back," he replied. "I started my own engineering company with a friend. We're 'Streeter and McMurtrie,'" he said proudly. "We've got the contract for laying the tracks from Glenwood to Aspen."

"The track laying went out on bid?" Luke asked, staring at McMurtrie, whose face was shadowed by the brim of his hat.

"*Everything* went out on bid," John replied with a shrug. "Excavation, bridge building, tracks, tunnels. Is that a problem?"

"Then why in blazes do they need a gang boss?" Luke was stunned! What gang was he supposed to lead?

"Ooohh," John said slowly. "You're replacing *Carpenter*. Well! I guess I have to agree a mite with Ricker. I'm a little suprised Moffat hired you, too."

"That's three of us then," Luke replied with disgust. He turned to watch the men tying Sneed's body over the mule he had tried to steal. Luke was wordless long enough that John felt the need to break the silence. "By the way, Luke, this here's Frank Kyner."

Luke turned to see the short, fair man being introduced. "Frank's company is handling the excavating for Division Three."

"So the construction is broken into divisions? That's probably a good idea," Luke said. He understood suddenly that Moffat and Jackson had really told him nothing about the construction at all. "You know, it'd probably be useful to meet with the heads of the contractors, just to understand the situation. Jackson and Moffat seemed to feel I would be able to speed the project along. But under the circumstances, I can't imagine how."

McMurtrie and Kyner looked at each other, pursing their lips in thought. "I suppose we might be able to introduce you," John said. "Most everyone has stopped for today here in the Second Division. We rode down to escort the paymasters to the Third. Have to finish the trip by wagon since the tracks aren't complete. You'd be welcome to come along. We're bunking here tonight and heading out in the morning."

Luke nodded agreement, then said with no small amount of frustration. "Maybe you could tell me where Ricker will be spending most of his time, so I can arrange not to be there. I've never been as good at holding my words as you, John. Frankly, I'd heard he would be in Denver and wouldn't bother us."

Frank Kyner barked a laugh. "Hardly! This has turned into his pet project. But he's spending most of his time in the Third Division with us. He probably won't bother you if you stay with your crews here in the cañon."

"And my crews are . . . ?" Luke asked.

"Let's get the boys together and talk over supper," McMurtrie said. "You may decide to go back to Denver, after all."

# CHAPTER 12

As Luke ate his pail of beans and bread, his first decision was to have a crew hunt game for the men. The camp at Dotsero was just outside the trainman's car, hundreds strong. It was the size of an army. An army travelled on its stomach. The men had to eat more food than beans and bread if they hoped to get the best work from them.

Despite the outside chill, the caboose was comfortable. A pot bellied stove in the corner radiated enough heat to warm the close quarters. Luke felt right at home. This car, like most of the "crew" cars, was built to make the most of a small space. It held both lower and upper seats, which could be reached by a ladder bolted directly to the wall. There were built-in cabinets with latches and a small, built-in desk and chair. He had crowded into the car with the other eight men. Since he was the last to enter, he sat at the desk and had to lean over and turn his head to see the men seated on the lower bench beside him. Luke planned to keep his eyes open and his mouth shut, so he could take measure of the men he'd be working with.

Seated between two men on one of the padded bunks, John started the introductions. "Luke, you'll be sharing a bunk car with Captain Ballard. Up on your right, Clyde Parker, foreman of the telegraph gang. And this is our chief engineer, John Morton." Luke nodded at each introduction. He heard a few "welcomes" and "howdy-dos." "Howard Ballard is probably the finest tunnel man in the western states and territories. He and Ed Rundell, Captain David Hanford and Philip Filius will be handling all the blasting and leveling in the big tunnel."

"Mr. Jackson indicated there would be four tunnels," Luke said. He set his pail on a small writing desk, painted green like everything else in the car. Luke looked up at the man introduced.

Howard looked down at Luke from his perch on a high riding chair across the aisle. He swallowed a bite of bread and corrected in a rolling bass, "Three full tunnels and one half tunnel-half-arch — ."

A sudden crash interrupted him. The entire train car shook from an impact. Plates and cups flew from hands, but the group quickly found their footing. They exited the car to find the camp engulfed in a fight.

"Rotten cheat!" exclaimed one big man, as he picked up a smaller man and again threw him into the side of the rail car.

Luke leapt into the battle and grabbed the aggressor in a head-lock. The man introduced as Captain Ballard also entered the fray and gripped the victim tightly to ensure that he wouldn't retaliate.

Ballard was a big man and held the much smaller man without effort. Ricker, John, and the others tended to similar battles throughout the camp. "I believe that you were asking about the tunnels, Colonel," Ballard said calmly. "The first, right above Cottonwood Falls, is where Dittmer's company will start. This train brought the equipment I'll need to start my own tunneling. I should be able to start next week." He ducked suddenly to avoid a flying coffeepot.

"He's pretty proud of that Norwalk compressor," commented the man introduced as Morton with a note of teasing in his voice. He sat on the back of a big Mexican, who struggled to unseat him.

"Those compressors are the only thing that will get you to Aspen on time, John!" Howard said strongly. He had grown tired of struggling with the man who leapt like a snared cottontail and was yelling names at the man Luke held. He removed one hand from the man and used his fist to knock the man squarely on the back of the neck. The worker dropped soundlessly to the ground. Luke pursed his lips. Not a bad idea. He tightened his hold on his charge's jugular and watched as the man slumped into unconsciousness. Then dragged the man a few feet and lowered him to the ground near a campfire. Ballard did likewise.

Dusting off his clothing, Howard turned to Luke. "I begged, borrowed, and sold what was left of my soul to get enough money to buy those two Norwalks," he said as though they had never been interrupted. "Finest in the world! I have eight Sargeant drills, powered with them. We'll drill into the rock in multiple locations, set blasting powder charges to fracture the center, then move forward and repeat the process. Colonel, your rock gang will muck out the material and haul it away. David Price's company will level the bench and handle the grading. I plan to move twenty feet a day, so we'll have to coordinate closely."

Luke raised his brows and let out a low whistle. "Pretty ambitious! You really think it'll go that fast?"

"Has to!" Howard replied. "The tracks must arrive in Glenwood Springs no later than October first. I have crews at work with hand drills right now, getting the face of the tunnel ready for the compressors. Once the tunnels are blasted, we'll have to level the bench inside and lay the track. The first two are little ones. Tunnel One is 290 feet. Dittmer should have that done in a few weeks. The second tunnel is only 133 feet. The third has a natural arch, so it'll only be a bit of blasting to make a short, half-tunnel."

"I really don't think that fourth tunnel is going to be as easy as you think," Morton said, shaking his head. "Oof!" He was finally unseated by his charge. "A little help here, fellows!"

"It's just granite," Ballard said as he reached out a big hand and found the back of the Mexican's shirt. "Length doesn't matter. I should have it done about the same time as Dittmer. He's using hand drills. My compressor will make short work of the blast holes."

Luke had tired of the battle. It seemed to be escalating instead of quieting. He pulled his sidearm and fired three shots into the air. Sound suddenly stopped all over camp. "That will be enough!!" Luke exclaimed in his best command voice, to Ballard's approving nod. "You men get to your tents *immediately*, or you'll be fired. You can find your own way back to Denver!"

Grumbling and nursing injuries, the men moved toward the long rows of tents. Morton looked at Howard and shook his head. "All I know is I've seen some odd stratas in this cañon. You could run into *anything* in thirteen hundred feet."

Luke holstered his Dragoon and dusted off his shirt. "Thirteen hundred feet! That's quite a tunnel!"

Howard set his jaw. "It's a tunnel, just like the others. We'll have it done on time!" His eyes flashed.

John joined the group. "Don't get excited, Howard. We all know that if any man alive can make that tunnel happen, it's you. Right, fellows?"

They all nodded until Ballard's countenance settled. In the caboose they took their places once more. An occasional loud shout made them keep one ear to the camp.

Harry Hurst spoke up from the second level across from Ballard. "I understand that you were recommended for this post by General Palmer, Colonel Ballister."

A small, rude sound came from a man in the corner near the stove. Harry ignored the comment and continued. "I've only been with the road for a year, so I never had the pleasure to meet the General. But John says my water service crew is in good hands."

"So the water service gang is under my command, as well as the rock gang?" Luke asked.

John nodded and took a gulp of fragrant black coffee. "And the telegraph gang. The telegraph gang are the only workers left in the First Division." At Luke's questioning look, John explained. "The First Division is from Red Cliff to the Eagle River. We're already done laying tracks in that section. The Second Division, from the river to

Satank, past Glenwood Springs, is working on laying track now. We're held up until the tunnels are in and leveled. Well, that and waiting for rail to arrive."

"What a *surprise* . . .," muttered John Morton snidely.

"I'm doing the best I can!" Colonel Ricker growled from the far end of the lower bunk. It was he who had made the rude noise earlier. Luke would have preferred to have the meeting without Ricker, but being on the far end of the car, opposite him, was the best he could do.

"Well, it's not good enough!" David Price said. "How many times do I have to order iron, Robert? And hay! My stock can't eat stone. There's not a single place to graze these animals. Why is it so dang hard to get supplies here?"

"There's a lot of stations between Denver and here," Ricker replied with frustration. "One thing goes wrong at one station, and the car ends up on a siding in Salida. I can't rightly be everywhere! I'm just as frustrated as the rest of you! I'm responsible to the president for this project. It's my career on the line!"

Luke could see the annoyance etched on the man's face. Much as he disliked Ricker, he could understand his frustration.

"Well, if the problem is with time, can we order more supplies than we need and store them on site?" Luke asked tentatively, even though he was certain the issue had been addressed long before he arrived.

"No room!" Ricker said.

"Is there room to build a siding here at Dotsero?" pressed Luke.

Ricker shook his head, but he was thinking now, not just defending himself. "Not without removing sleeping quarters. The men are already three to a tent. We'd lose probably ten tents to a siding."

"Are there enough bunk cars in the system that can be brought here? We can fit eight per car if the men double up on the bunks — ten if we use the floor," Luke continued.

Shouts and curses outside informed those in the car that the workers had resumed their gambling. Luke knew that another battle loomed on the horizon.

Ricker looked startled, then pursed his lips and thought for a moment. "They're building an expansion down south, but they don't have the space limitations of our spur. I might be able to convince John Connell to move some bunk cars up here. That'd free up enough space. We could move the bunk cars out of the way when supplies arrived."

"It's worth a try," McMurtrie said, brightening considerably. "If we could secure the bunk cars now, they'd be available when we start laying the Third Division, from Satank to Aspen. There's *no* room for tents up the Roaring Fork."

Ricker was nodding to himself with a small smile, not looking at Luke. "Connell might do it on my say-so. It could work out quite nicely for me." He said it under his breath but Luke heard it.

"*Just like Ricker,*" Luke thought, "*Always looking to step up in the organization — on the backs of his fellows.*" Still, if the line arrived in Aspen on time they would all be well rewarded. He decided to hold his tongue for the time being.

"Any word on the Midland?" Morton asked Ricker.

"They just completed their only tunnel on Hagerman Pass," Colonel Ricker replied with annoyance. "With good weather, they might reach Aspen by the second week of November."

"I thought we had until Christmas, Robert!" McMurtrie exclaimed. The startled, concerned looks from the rest made Luke wonder what the stakes of this race really were.

"Their tunnel went quicker than our spies expected," Ricker replied. "We'll just have to move faster."

"We're already pushing the men to exhaustion," David Price said. "Our only hope is to pay them more."

Luke spoke up. "I've requested Moffat and Jackson approve a pay raise when we reach Glenwood. I was afraid there'd be a great number of walk-outs when the men reached the first civilization they'd seen in a year."

David nodded. Harry Hurst looked pleased. Ricker looked annoyed, but didn't comment.

John reached into his jacket and checked a silver pocket watch. He stretched his back and wiped a speck of sauce from his mustache. "I think we should call it a night, gentlemen. Tomorrow will be here soon and we need to get an early start to get the pay wagon to the Third Division."

Luke checked his own watch and was startled at the hour. John was right. Daylight would be fast upon them and he was anxious to see the rest of the project. He was beginning to see how he could help the Denver & Rio Grande win the race!

# CHAPTER 13

Morning found Luke in a wagon with the pay crew and the locked strong box of gold. Frank Kyner took the lead on his pale mule. McMurtrie and Ricker took the rear. The regular stage route over Cottonwood Pass was unusable because of the spring thaws, so they headed north over the Carbonate Trail. A private toll road at the old town of Carbonate would take them to Glenwood Springs, and then they would travel up the Roaring Fork Valley to the Third Division camp. They talked while the mules pulled the heavy wagon up the steep trail.

Luke learned that the ties for the line were being made on site. There was a small mill that the road had commandeered for the project, up No Name Creek. With the abundance of pine trees on the mountainside, a crew was sawing enough ties to keep up with construction. They were rough-hewn, with no protective coating, but speed was the issue here. The company could re-build later, when there was the time, and the income from tourists and ore.

A rough bridge had been constructed over the river near the area called Shoshone Falls. The City of Glenwood Springs was constructing a water works project in the location. They would be able to use the bridge to move men and materials to begin blasting the west side of the fourth tunnel.

"I know you three have been working primarily in the Third Division, but do you have any idea why production has slowed in the cañon?" Luke asked over an early lunch. The animals were taking a much-needed break at the town of Carbonate. Leaving before dawn had ensured that they would reach Glenwood Springs that same day, but they were hungry early, as well.

"Two problems that I've seen, Luke," McMurtrie said between bites of bread, "are the heavy drinkers that you can't roust in the morning, and the supply problem we've already discussed."

"Don't begin that argument again, John," warned Ricker.

"I'm not starting anything, Robert," McMurtrie replied. "It doesn't matter where the fault lies. The simple fact is that supplies have been delayed beyond all reason. No matter what the train schedule is in the southern divisions, it should not take eight days for a load of grain to reach the front from Westcliffe!"

Ricker sighed and nodded his head. "Agreed. I've tried to explain to the management that a substitute supply for most things is not available in this location. They don't seem to listen."

Luke found the exchange interesting. That John McMurtrie and Robert Ricker would agree on *anything* was amazing enough, but it seemed to Luke that Ricker was actually trying to make the project succeed.

After paying the toll, the wagon and riders headed south toward Glenwood. The route was circuitous. Once the mud hardened in the sun, Cottonwood Pass would be a much more direct route to the camp.

"What is the total manpower for the three divisions?" Luke asked.

Ricker replied. He seemed to be growing accustomed to Luke's questions, and while certainly not warm, he was at least civil in his responses. "Nearly one thousand men, and six hundred draft animals."

"Is there any way to start constructing rail in the Third Division while the Second Division is still building?"

Frank Kyner shook his head. "We're already surveying, excavating, and building whatever trestles are needed. But the sheer volume of rails and ties that will be needed are too bulky to move by wagon."

"Is there a mill on that end of the valley?" Luke continued.

"No," Ricker said. "But the mill at No Name Creek is keeping up with construction so far. They should be able to continue that progress, so long as we continue to supply them with new blades."

They rode long hours before the mountains opened to reveal the Glenwood Springs Valley. Perfect as a dream but cut off from the world, the little town was nearly frantic to receive either the Rio Grande or the Midland line. Even with the long stage route, tourists flocked to the health "sanitarium" of Glenwood, famous for the Yampah Vapor Caves and hot mineral baths.

"We'll need to stop off at the Sheriff's office," Kyner said. "Got word before we left that a couple of men had been arrested for a bar brawl. Figured they could stay right where they were until we returned."

"Jack Carney is a D&RG man, but Dave Frazer is mine," McMurtrie said. "Luke, you should probably go introduce yourself to the saloonkeep, Joe Bart. You'll find a lot of the men in the Third wander down to Glenwood in the night, and wind up sleeping off a bottle on the bar floor. Robert, could you come with me to fetch your man?"

When Ricker nodded, McMurtrie turned back to Luke. "Meet me at the Sheriff's office and I'll introduce you there."

Luke shook his head. "John, if I'm going to keep up production in the cañon, how am I going to watch the men working in this division? I'd be on the road every other day." When McMurtrie only shrugged, Luke turned his attention. "You willing to take care of this end of the valley, Colonel Ricker?"

"I am general superintendent and chief engineer of all of the D&RG, Colonel Ballister," Ricker replied arrogantly. "I have concerns of my own. I'm overseeing the surveying, planning the route for this expansion, and ensuring that the trains can handle the grade. I'm also corresponding with the southern expansion, and *attempting* to keep up with my duties in Denver. I could barely afford the time to escort the pay wagon. *You* are the gang boss. You'll have to find a way. Carpenter did."

"If Carpenter had *found* a way," Luke replied coldly, "I wouldn't have been hired." He shook his head again. "I'll need to delegate something or I'll be no use to anyone."

Ricker shrugged. "Take whatever action you feel is required, so long as it doesn't increase *my* duties." He turned his mule and trotted toward the Sheriff's office. Luke could only stare, frustrated beyond belief, at the retreating form.

Frank Kyner spoke after a moment. "Luke, that wagon across the street is the road's. You can pick up the animals we boarded down at the livery. I'll check the saloon for stragglers. Meet me over there with the wagon and we can head up."

Luke nodded and walked down to the livery stable at the end of Grand Avenue. Two braying burros were brought to him, and he signed his name on the ticket that would be sent to Denver for payment. He hitched the animals and drove to the saloon.

Joe Bart was not a large man. He was polite and well-spoken, but was frustrated with the railroad men. They had money, but few manners. He was often forced to throw them out, or serve them until they passed out so they wouldn't break up the place. One or two had been rough with the girls upstairs and he had been forced to call the Sheriff.

Two of Kyner's men were passed out in the corner, sleeping off a night of carousing. Luke tried to rouse them, without success. He took one and Frank picked up the other. They went outside and tossed them in the wagon.

"Colonel Ballister?" the owner asked. "They didn't pay for their last round."

Luke stared at him incredulously. "Are you expecting the road to pay you??"

"Well no, I suppose not," Joe replied slowly, "But is there any chance you can dock their pay or something? You know. For good town relations?"

Luke sighed. Public relations was not his strong point. He understood that every time the railroad reached a new town, the owners tried to make sure the townsfolk were appeased for the inconvenience of the construction and future operations. He reached into a pocket and extracted a silver dollar. "This cover it?" he asked the owner.

"Oh, more than enough! Yes, sir!" Bart replied. "I really appreciate the trouble, Colonel. If I can be of any help in the future, you let me know."

As Luke turned away, time froze. A vision of loveliness was talking to the owner of the grocery. Blonde hair the color of summer sunshine, eyes as blue as cornflowers. She almost took his breath away. With a pale gingham bonnet and matching winter dress, her graceful young form couldn't help but draw his stare. He tipped his hat when he caught her eye, but she quickly disappeared into the store.

"Excuse me, Sir," came a female voice to his left. He turned to see an older woman in a dark brown dress and hat. "If you're Colonel Ballister, then the gentleman on the horse over there said I should talk to you."

Luke turned to see Ricker flashing an evil grin as he trotted away on his mule. Wonderful! Now what!

# Chapter 14

The saloon was across the street from Mr. Putman's dry goods. It was nearly dark and Maribelle was delivering a crock of pickles she and her mother had cured all winter with dill, garlic, and onions. Mr. Putman had slowly inhaled the spicy fragrance and fished into the crock to pluck out the largest cucumber. After he took a crunchy bite, he smiled, and agreed to buy the lot. She and her mother had hoped to trade the sour treats for thread and cloth to make new summer dresses.

Maribelle had looked longingly at the pretty store-bought dresses near the doorway, her nose nearly pressed to the patterned cloth to see the stitching. The style of the dress was a soft blur, like everything else in her life. Just short of blind since she was a young child, her life wasn't easy. She often made mistakes and was frequently clumsy. Still, Mama and Papa tried to be patient. She tried hard to remember the design of the dress, so she could duplicate it at home.

As she studied the dress, a wagon pulled up directly in front of her. Maribelle stopped to watch a blonde man step down from the high wooden seat into the street. She heard two harnessed burros braying restlessly. Their bobbing heads jingled the metal of their bits and chin chains. The man patted the neck of the nearest animal lightly on his way past and the animal settled a bit. He stalked into the saloon with an air of command. His movements almost forced a person to watch him. This was no boy like those she had attended school with.

She could hear voices coming from behind the swinging doors of the Silver Nugget. Maribelle had never seen the inside of the saloon. Even the women who *worked* there weren't allowed to enter. It was likely that the interior of the Silver Nugget would forever remain a mystery to her.

As she watched, the owner of the saloon and another man accompanied the blonde man out onto the shadowed main street. The blonde and the other man each carried the inert form of a drunken man. They tossed them into the wagon with the same ease her father tossed a bale of hay to the horses.

Joe Bart, the Silver Nugget's owner, and the blonde man watched the drunk men clumsily climb further into the rear of the wagon.

"I appreciate your not calling the Sheriff, Mr. Bart," the blonde man said in a medium baritone. The voice had a cultured edge that seemed foreign in this rough country. The voice interested Maribelle. It had confidence, strength, and polish. He stood with his boots planted firmly on the boardwalk, arms crossed on his chest. He didn't offer to help the drunk men the rest of the way into the wagon, and when she squinted, Maribelle could just make out the small, dark pleasure he took in their struggle.

"They didn't cause no trouble, Colonel," the owner of the saloon said in his usual light tenor. Oh! A colonel. No wonder he seemed commanding. The owner continued, "Just sat in the corner and slept it off. They didn't even know when I closed down for the night."

"Nor when you opened for the morning, apparently," the Colonel said with disapproval.

Maribelle couldn't hear the next exchange, but she heard the Colonel sigh, saw him shake his head and reach into a pocket. He handed the saloon owner a coin. When the two men were seated unsteadily in the wagon, the Colonel turned to enter the saloon a second time.

"Maribelle," Mr. Putman called from the store, "I've got your total ready." The Colonel glanced up when he heard the voice. The men in the wagon did as well. The blonde man's eyes locked on hers, and he smiled and tipped his hat. She felt herself blush to the roots of her hair! She turned quickly and entered the store.

When she emerged several minutes later, she was surprised to see her mother, of all people, talking with the blonde man on the opposite side of the street! Maribelle stood self-consciously on the plank sidewalk, not sure whether to approach. The Colonel's eyes lighted on her as she stood in the sunlight and he gave her a warm smile.

Her mother noticed his attention shift, and her eyes lighted on Maribelle.

"Maribelle, come over here, please."

"Yes, Mama," she said, as softly as the distance would allow. She felt her heart beat faster as she approached. She was struggling with a basket, filled with supplies, and had a bag of flour in her other arm. She didn't see the edge of the planked sidewalk and fell face down right near the wagon with the drunk men.

"Well, well! What a purty little thing *you* are!" exclaimed the heavyset white man closest to her. "Just you stay right where you are and I'll join you. That's right where I *like* a woman!"

Maribelle felt her face redden. The other man whistled and hooted and made other, ruder, comments.

She scurried to pick up the scattered supplies before the men had time to move toward her. She felt like a clumsy oaf, and her knee hurt. She had banged it right on the edge of the wood. She felt like crying.

As she picked up the last apple, a quiet baritone voice sounded next to her. "That will be *enough*!" The words were spoken quietly, but they carried a weight, a sharpness that could cut stone. The men silenced so suddenly that it startled her. Maribelle saw a hand reach down, palm out. She glanced up and found herself staring into the deep green eyes of the blonde man, close enough that she could see the details of his face. She blushed again. She couldn't help it. Lord, but he was handsome!

She took the offered hand and felt the controlled strength in his arms as he helped her to her feet. He held her hand gently and only provided assistance and balance.

Maribelle felt the annoyed eyes of the men in the wagon full on her back. She didn't dare turn around for fear of starting the comments a second time.

When she was standing, he picked up the flour so she would have a hand free, and offered his arm. She slipped her arm into the crook of his and was surprised when he squeezed it lightly against his body.

As she walked arm in arm with the stranger to where her mother stood, the man spoke to her in a low voice, so only she could hear. "I apologize for the conduct of my men, Miss. I'm afraid they've been outside of civilization long enough they've forgotten how to speak to a proper lady."

Maribelle found herself smiling in spite of herself. She had never considered herself a "proper lady."

"That's all right," she replied quietly. "I probably deserved it, for being so clumsy."

He stopped suddenly, before they reached her mother. He turned toward her and said quietly but very seriously, "No woman deserves to be subjected to comments like that. No matter *what* their actions." Maribelle didn't know how to respond and just looked at him curiously before he smiled again and led her to her mother.

# CHAPTER 15

An hour later, Luke trotted beside John McMurtrie on Kyner's mule so Frank could stay in the wagon with his men. They could see it behind them in the distance, moving slowly over the rough ground. The spectacular beauty of the valley was breathtaking. The Roaring Fork River cascaded over rocks to their right, and the breeze blew chilled cañon air up to them. The construction front of the third division spread before them. Excavation had occurred as far as Satank, and the surveyors were marking the route between Emma and Snowmass. They watched as men with wheelbarrows removed stone and red soil from a cut in the mountainside. A team of Belgians dragged a boulder away from the grade.

"Who was the woman Ricker sent over to you?" John asked.

"Mrs. Bert Johnson," Luke replied, fighting to get the image of the young daughter's soft blue eyes from his mind. "Husband's an old road employee who's been abed for some time. She and her daughter take in mending. She wanted to know if anyone in the Third needed rips mended or socks darned. Penny an item."

"What's the husband's trouble?" John asked as he slowed his mount.

"A green yearling threw him and trampled him pretty bad," Luke replied, slowing his mule to a walk.

"So his wife and daughter have to support him?" John asked, shaking his head sadly. "That's a right shame."

Luke responded as casually as he could. "Told her I'd check around and perhaps drop by some mending on my way back to the Second."

John looked at him and responded with a sly smile. "Think you'd be going to the trouble if the daughter wasn't so pretty?"

Luke winced inwardly, but said with a touch of accusation. "I'm trying to help out an old roadhand. We stick together, don't we?"

" 'Course we do, Luke," John said with twinkling eyes, " 'Course we do." He spurred his animal to a startled canter, leaving Luke behind.

"Just helping an old roadhand," Luke repeated softly to himself. He tried to believe it.

Colonel Ricker was talking to a tall, heavy-set man. The man was punctuating his words with wild hand movements. Ricker motioned

Luke over. Luke glanced over to where John was dismounting and talking to another fellow, probably his project lieutenant.

"Something you need, Colonel?" Luke asked politely when he reached the pair.

"Frank, this is Colonel Luke Ballister, the new gang boss. I can't help you, but he probably can." There was a dark twinkling in Ricker's eyes that Luke remembered well. Luke knew Ricker wasn't going to overstep his bounds by making him perform jobs outside his scope, but neither would he be helpful. Luke would earn his pay on this assignment — he could see the signs.

The man stuck out a meaty hand. "Frank King, Colonel. I'm the assistant chief engineer for this division." Luke shook the powerful hand without outwardly showing the effort.

"I need you to assign John Morton to the Third for two weeks or so."

Luke furrowed his brow. "John's not available right now. They're just starting the tunnels. He'll be needed to plan the route and oversee the blasting."

"I understand that, Colonel, but this is an emergency!" King responded with movements so broad that Luke's mule flattened its ears and began to prance.

"What's the trouble?" he asked.

"Sabotage!" King exclaimed in a loud voice. Silence descended on the men working around them, and Luke shut his eyes for a moment and sighed. Even Ricker's eyes went wide, and he glanced around him, annoyed.

"Keep it down!" Ricker hissed, dismounting and moving King to the side so the animals blocked their conversation. Luke likewise swung from his mount. He turned to the men who had fallen silent and said, "You men get back to work!" Only after the workers reluctantly returned to their duties did he turn his attention to King and Ricker.

Ricker kept his hand on King's arm, probably to prevent it from hitting his face when it began to gesture again. "Now, what's this about sabotage, Frank? Are you sure?"

"Couldn't be anything else," King responded. "All my survey stakes are gone! The whole route to Snowmass had been glassed and staked, and now they're gone! Every blasted one of them!"

"Could they have blown away, or animals rooted them up?" Luke asked reasonably.

King's eyes flashed. "I know how to pound stakes, Colonel. They're not just displaced. They're flat gone! Holes covered over so's you wouldn't even know where they'd been. I have my transit and grade notebooks, but I need someone to help me put the stakes back. It took me three weeks with a couple of men to chart that route. It'll take that long again if I have to do it myself. The construction will be to Emma in a week. I need someone who's good with the equipment — and won't break it — to help me."

The engineer was right. The equipment was delicate and easy to damage. No replacements would be available in the field. Luke agreed that someone with the necessary skill was required, but they couldn't afford to lose Morton for two weeks or more. Then it hit him! A smile lit Luke's face. Ricker frowned, his eyes taking on a wary look.

"Mr. King, I'll be honest. I really can't afford to lose Morton for that long, but I do have a solution." Luke said, trying to keep a straight face.

Ricker's eyes narrowed, but they also held a level of uncertainty.

"Frank," Luke said, casually putting an arm across his shoulders, "you're in luck! You've got, right here with you, the chief engineer of all of the D&RG! He was just mentioning to me earlier that he was very concerned about making sure the survey to Aspen was correct. I feel *certain* your emergency could be handled by his superior skills." Luke smiled at Ricker.

King's broad face suddenly glowed with pleasure. "You're absolutely right! I had forgotten Colonel Ricker was an engineer!" He turned his delighted countenance to Robert Ricker. "I'm confident that with no more than seven long days of hard work, the two of us can have the route marked again. I'm pleased I don't have to inform Denver of a delay to the project."

"Yes, of course," Ricker said slowly, glaring daggers at Luke, who smiled contentedly. "We'll get started tomorrow morning, Frank."

King turned to Luke and smiled. He took one of Luke's hands in both of his and pumped it again and again. "Thank you so much for the excellent solution, Colonel Ballister!"

"Oh, yes, Colonel," Ricker commented, "thank you *so much* for your idea."

Luke was chuckling to himself when he again found John McMurtrie.

"What was that I heard about sabotage?" John asked softly.

"Someone took up all the survey stakes from Emma to Snowmass," Luke responded. "Probably Midland spies."

John shook his head and leaned closer to Luke. "Couple of my men were in town last night. They saw a table of men. The boys didn't say anything to them, but noticed there were shovels under the table with fresh dirt. Ernest said he saw the stamp of the Union Pacific."

Luke shook his head. He should have known there would be opposition from all sides. He would have to be especially careful in his division. He remembered the missing grain.

After the pay was made to the crew, Luke sat down to dinner with the heads of the Third Division contractors. The walls of the thick canvas command tent billowed and snapped in the near-constant breeze. The tent stove made the interior almost uncomfortably warm. Luke sat on the tent floor where the air was a bit cooler. Once again, John made introductions. He concluded with, "Luke, Al Clark here is my second lieutenant and of course, you know Frank King," John said. King tipped his hat and smiled. "His brother, Charles," John continued, "runs the engineering department in Denver."

"Who has the contracts up here for building?" Luke asked.

"Well, obviously, Streeter & McMurtrie is laying track. My lieutenant is Bill McLeod. You'll probably talk to him more than to me. I send him to Glenwood to send telegrams, and to the Second to coordinate construction. Joseph Carroll with Franklin & Carroll is overseeing grading. You've already met Frank Kyner, handling excavation, and Will Marshall of Billings & Gunn is taking care of bridge couplings and sidings."

"Don't forget Allender," Kyner said in a soft tenor.

"Oh, yes!" replied John. "Allender is your animal handler in the Third. Does a splendid job with the draft teams."

Allender spoke up from the center, where he was leaning on a support pole near the stove. "You're the new gang boss? Good! See if you can convince Denver to ship hay and grain on time! Look at the countryside! What little grazing is here belongs to the ranchers, and they don't take kindly to grazing our stock on their land. I'm still waiting for a shipment of grain that was supposed to come in on this train!"

Luke responded. "I don't know about past shipments, but I can tell you that grain was loaded on the train at Gypsum. Ten sacks were stolen from the boxcar when we stopped, just before Dotsero."

Alarmed looks went around the room. "Any clue on the identity of the bandits?"

Luke shook his head. "Only that they managed to make off with the ten in less than five minutes. That's a little more coordinated than just a greedy farmer."

"Not the first time, either!" Ricker said. "We'll need to start posting guards. We've got enemies, gentlemen, make no mistake! They'll see us fail if we don't use caution."

"Do we need to go back to using coded transmissions, like we did during the Royal Gorge Wars?" Clark asked. Luke looked at him hard, then realized he did remember Clark manning the barricade at Cañon City. He thought coding was unnecessary in the present situation, but that was Ricker's decision.

"For the moment, I'll say no," Ricker replied after a moment of contemplation. "We might consider it if we run into situations where a simple delay could be utilized by our enemies to completely halt our progress. However, use discretion, gentlemen, when speaking to your men. The fewer people who know of the actual status of the construction, the better." Men nodded all around the tent.

In the morning, Luke was assigned a sleek brown mule mare. It so resembled his quarter horse that he renamed the animal "Star." Allender had no objections when he saw that the mule responded to the word as though it had been named at birth. He made note of the new designation in his records.

Luke was ready to return to the Second when he suddenly remembered the mending for the Johnson ladies. In a few minutes, he'd collected a number of items.

As promised, Luke stopped at the small Johnson house at the edge of Glenwood Springs to deliver the mending. He was a little alarmed at his disappointment that Miss Maribelle wasn't at home. Although Mrs. Johnson had only requested a penny an item, Luke had told the men two cents. The price had still been eagerly agreed to. Luke presented Mrs. Johnson with a shiny silver dollar — payment in advance. She was nearly beside herself with gratitude and assured Luke that the mending would be done without fail before he returned the following Saturday.

Although it would be difficult, Luke decided he would visit the Third Division once each week. Until the telegraph lines were run to the construction front, he would be unaware of the progress unless he visited the site.

He rested his mule again at the town of Carbonate, where he ate a bite of lunch. He could hear the first echoing of blasting powder long before he reached the Second Division. Howard Ballard was overseeing the hand drilling on the big, fourth tunnel as Luke rode up. He was speaking quickly to a slender Chinese man with straight black bangs over dark almond eyes. A wide brimmed leather hat seemed too large for his face. Ballard looked up as Luke dismounted. "Luke, come over here!"

"I heard the blasting, Howard," Luke said in greeting. He bowed his head a bit to the new Chinese man. "Starting the big tunnel?"

Ballard nodded. "Getting the rock face ready now. I want to be in a position to move in the equipment with no delay. Luke, this is Li Sung, my headman for the blasting crew. Li, this is Colonel Luke Ballister. He's the new gang boss for the railroad."

Li Sung bowed low before Luke. "Most pleased to meet you, honorable Boss," he said in stinted English.

Howard rolled his eyes. "Stow the 'honorable boss' line, Li. Just talk normal."

Li's eyes crinkled at the corners, and he smiled, showing wide teeth. "My apologies, Captain Ballard," he said in perfect English with a heavy British accent. He nodded at Luke. "And to you, Colonel Ballister. But many of the men become disturbed when I use the Queen's English."

Howard turned to Luke. "Li's father was a British schoolmaster; his mom a Chinese interpreter. His real name is 'Leland Edward Granger.' Speaks English, Chinese, Mandarin, and a couple of those other Eastern tongues. He uses a Chinese name on the pay rolls, so nobody asks questions. Also reads and writes — but don't tell anyone," he said as an aside.

Luke's eyebrows raised. Howard was right. A Celestial who could read and write, when many of the men couldn't, might end up hurt. "Glad to meet you, Li," he said.

The men behind Ballard had rolled a barrel of blasting powder close to the rock face. They began to ram the raw powder into the first hole, using a long wooden rod. Scoop and push, over and over.

"Howard, Li, we need to start to coordinate our wor . . .," began Luke, when a sudden explosion broke the air, following quickly by a scream of pain.

"Bloody hell!" Li exclaimed. He turned with blinding speed and rushed with Luke and Howard toward the mountain face.

One of the Mongolians was on the ground. Luke could see immediately what had happened. Something had sparked, and exploded the powder. The explosion had caused the rod to propel backward and impale the worker through the shoulder. His screams of pain were second only to those of another man sitting on the ground, hands over his face. Regardless of the language, Luke knew swearing when he heard it.

He watched as the big redhead turned to the accident. The Irishman muttered something and shook his head before returning to work.

Another man Luke recognized from the night before, one of the Chinese cooks, rushed forward holding one of the big pipes he'd seen

Chinese workers smoking on past jobs. A wisp of smoke rose from the contraption. He spoke first with the man holding his face. He had him remove his hands. The skin was raw and bloody. After a brief conversation and what appeared to be several brief tests, he moved to the impaled man. Blood poured from the wound, drenching the man's shirt and the grey dust underfoot.

"This is our herbalist — a doctor," Li said, at the questioning glance from Luke. The doctor knelt beside the man and began to speak low and earnestly. The wounded man nodded, trembling from the pain. He took the tube of the pipe between his lips and began to inhale slowly and deeply. After a few moments, he closed his eyes. The doctor checked his pulse in his neck, and then lifted an eyelid and peered inside. His hands moved with quick confidence.

"*Definitely a doctor,*" Luke thought.

At a gesture from the doctor, two men held the wounded man while another quickly pulled out the rod. Luke couldn't understand it — the man hardly moved, and uttered no sound. The men holding the injured man lowered him slowly to the ground. The doctor spent some time checking the wound and then came over to speak with Li. The words were low and serious and sounded like some language other than Chinese. Li nodded more than once and asked several questions in the same language. The doctor bowed low before Li, and scurried to order the men to attend the wounded man.

Li turned to Howard and Luke. "I'm quite sorry for the inconvenience, Captain," he said. "But it seems this worker has broken his collarbone. He will live, but it will take many days to heal. He will not be able to work the drill for you."

"Blast it!" Howard exclaimed. "I need every man I have. What about that one over there?" he asked, pointing to the rocking man.

"The herbalist says his face was injured by the powder. However, he can see from both eyes, and speak. Lin will tend him after he has made the other comfortable in his tent."

Howard and Luke walked back toward Luke's mule, leaving Li to get the crew back to work. As they passed Edward, they heard him mutter a comment. "Wouldn't a happened had he padded the rod."

Howard stopped and turned. "What did you say, Irishman?" he ordered.

Luke turned as well, to see Edward's face turn red. He lapsed into silence and lowered his head.

Ballard put a hand on Edward's huge arm and turned him. "I asked you what you said!" His eyes flashed.

"Let me handle this, Howard," Luke said, walking forward. He stepped over a pile of rubble that was being broken into ballast. "It's Edward, isn't it?"

Edward turned green eyes to the man who had tried to help him — who had threatened both Sneed and Carpenter and lived to speak of it. "Aye," he responded.

"What did you say just now as we walked by? Something about the rod?"

Edward shook his head. "The powder wouldn't a sparked had the Celestial padded the rod."

"It's a wooden dowel," Howard said strongly, "They don't spark!"

"And I'm to suppose it's not blood on the ground, then?" Edward asked with raised brows. Luke bit his lip so he wouldn't laugh.

Howard stopped and nearly smiled. "How would you know about blasting powder, and why would you say that the rod should be padded?" he asked quietly after a moment.

"Me Da' was a blaster," Edward said. "Built the Hoosac Tunnel, he did, for the Boston & Maine back in the '50s."

"They used nitroglycerine for that tunnel," Ballard said suspiciously, "Not powder." Luke was not familiar with the project so he left the conversation to the two.

"Not at first," said Edward. "Didn't bring in the nitro until later. Tried a great many things on that job, they did," he continued. "Even used a drilling machine — a 'mole' they called it, but they couldn't make it work."

Howard was beginning to nod his head. "I heard about that machine. Didn't know they used powder, though."

"The nitro, it was faster. They always wanted faster," Edward said with a sad shake of his head. "Me Da' died in a nitro explosion."

"Sorry," Howard said.

Luke nodded his sympathy as well. "How did you learn blasting?" he asked.

Edward shrugged. "Da' talked on visits. The job went on for years. He came home a few times. Excited to be on the project, he was. Always wanted to explain how the work was done. They padded the dowel with rifle wads — but of course, those were easy to find back then. Covered it with some damp linen."

Howard shook his head. "That'd wet the powder," he said. "Wouldn't work."

"I said *damp*, not wet," Edward said, with sarcasm in his voice. "There'd be no more moisture than the air we breathe."

Howard was unaccustomed to being spoken to as an equal by a gandy dancer. His eyes narrowed briefly, but then he nodded his head thoughtfully.

"Have you worked with blasting powder yourself?" Ballard asked.

"Aye," Edward responded. "A bit, in the silver mines in Leadville. Liked it well enough, but the road was paying better."

Howard turned to Luke. "He making standard wage?"

Luke shrugged. A breeze had sprung up and his nose filled with the scent of gun powder. "Don't really know," he said. "I'd have to check the pay rolls, but I suppose so."

Howard turned to Edward. "You be interested in working with my blasting gang? Pay's good."

Luke's eyebrows nearly disappeared under his hat, while Edward's mouth opened in disbelief. "Think that's wise, Howard?" Luke asked cautiously. "The Irish and the Celestials aren't known for getting on. And what about the languages?"

"I work with my crews, and I don't speak the language," Ballard said with the beginnings of annoyance. "That's why I have a headman. And as for getting on, they're paid to work, not socialize." Howard gestured for Li Sung to join them. "Li, any problems with hiring this Irishman for the crew?"

The Chinese weren't known for much expression, so the widened eyes told Luke a great deal. He looked at Edward, trying to place him, then nodded. "I believe the crew will work with this man," he said with confidence. "He was accused wrongly and bore the lash with no sound. We watched, and the men believed his actions showed courage and honor."

Edward's face showed surprise. "I make good pay with the road," he said to Ballard. He had to think of his family. With Tommy gone, he would be supporting his sister's family, as well.

Howard crossed his arms over his chest and adjusted his position on the rocks. "I'll pay you $90 per month, and I'll reimburse the road for your food and whiskey."

"Begorry!" Edward exclaimed. The increased pay would almost replace Tommy's income. "Would I have to sleep with the others?"

Howard shook his head. "I haven't an extra tent, and I don't suppose the D&RG will let you stay put."

"We're three to a tent now," Luke said with a shake of his head. "We need the space." The breeze was becoming a wind. Luke nearly lost his hat in a sudden gust. He glanced upward to see the sky darkening. He'd need to get the mule unsaddled and brushed before the rain started.

Li spoke up. "I would share my tent with this man," he said calmly.

"Satisfactory," Howard said. "As the headman, Li bunks alone. That'll be fine with me. Finish out your day with the road, and report to Li in the morning."

Edward looked taken aback, but recovered quickly. "I suppose I'll be getting back to work, then."

"I'll wire Denver to remove him from our rolls and write his final check," Luke said, and moved to pick up Star's reins. Rain began to patter down on his shoulders as he watched the big Irishman pick up his hammer, still shaking his head in disbelief at the turn of events.

# CHAPTER 16

The weeks flew by in frantic activity. Up at dawn, work until dusk, with paperwork late into the night. It was three in the morning by Luke's watch when he finished the weekly pay reports and wrote his status memo to Denver. He quietly slipped out of the chair while the others slept, and added a few lumps of coal to the stove.

Luke raised his arms above his head to stretch his back, and yawned. The last of the coffee, now thick and strong, was poured into his cup. He set the empty pot on the floor so it wouldn't burn. Staring out the small window nearby, he noted that one or two of the tents still had a lantern burning. He would remember to take special care to roust those men at dawn and confirm they were sober enough to work. After yesterday morning's incident, he was going to check on anyone who didn't appear in control. Drunken men wouldn't be allowed to work on the cliff face any more.

Poor Mickey Murray! He'd been old for the rock gang — more than fifty-five, according to his fellows. He'd stayed up drinking too long the night before. His crew had crossed the river at Shoshone, and started up the path to where Ballard's partner, Philip Filius, was pushing the western head of the tunnel. It was only five in the morning, and black as pitch. Mickey had taken the wrong path, and wound up stumbling right off the cliff face into the Grand River. After an hour of searching the banks of the fast-moving water, they'd been forced to give up. Luke had been tasked with notifying his family in New York City.

He was frustrated and angry. He hated to lose a man to such a needless accident. In the morning, he'd get a crew over to the western face to mark the proper path.

Lord, but he was tired! Still, progress had been good. It was already summer, and three of the tunnels were completed. Dittmer was rightfully proud of his second tunnel, a quarter mile above Cottonwood Falls. Luke had to admit it was a pretty thing. A famous photographer named Jackson had visited the site, and both Dittmer and Ballard were delighted that he took some plates of the tunnels, surrounded by the crews. Luke couldn't imagine why anyone would be interested in a picture of a construction crew, but some people had odd tastes.

In just a few days, it would be Independence Day. Several of the men had demanded that work stop for the holiday. Luke shook his head incredulously as he took a last sip of coffee and prepared for bed. What a ridiculous notion! Howard said he would have his blasting crew make some sky rockets, and that settled the men a bit. Luke stripped to his union suit, and put out the soft glow of the lantern. Darkness settled around him like a warm glove.

He lay down and pulled the blanket over him, thinking briefly about how far they'd come since he arrived in April. Luke didn't see any reason why they couldn't reach Glenwood by September, and Aspen the following month. Of course, it depended on the tunnels. Howard was making excellent time on the last tunnel, designated the Jackson Tunnel in honor of the outgoing president. Progress was so good that Luke's rock gang was struggling to keep up with mucking out the material. Many of the men were complaining they were overworked and asked for a larger crew. The road actually was trying to bring in more men, but even with increased wages, there were few applying. Luke hadn't realized until he heard the men's comments, how much of the work Edward had done.

Luke continued to muse. Edward seemed to be working well with the Celestials. They didn't speak much, but Luke had heard laughter coming from the tent Edward and Li shared, on more than one occasion. It surprised him a bit.

"*Moffat's another surprise,*" Luke thought with a small smile. He was pushing construction forward on all fronts in a manner that reminded Luke forcibly of the General, and was working on an advertising campaign to lure new tourists to the scenic wonders of Colorado, and especially Glenwood Springs and Aspen. Word down the line was that people were already slavering to ride the train — before it was even finished!

Luke turned toward the wall and tried to quiet his thoughts, to no avail. He and the others still struggled with the problems of construction. Supply deficits and mistakes were on-going. Twice Denver had forwarded thirty pound steel instead of the fifty-two pound they were using for the rails. Thirty pound was fine for sidings, but wouldn't hold up under constant wear. The forty pound being torn up from the failed southern expansions had been barely acceptable as a substitute, but last month they'd had to return five cars of iron and wait for new.

After a conversation with John Morton and Colonel Ricker, they'd decided to forego fishplates in the cañon. They couldn't seem to get an adequate supply and simply didn't have time to wait.

Luke turned on his back. He must get some sleep! The stove hissed in the background. A wind was coming up outside. It sang through the trees and rustled the tents. Howard turned on his bunk above Luke and the springs creaked annoyingly.

Everything was annoying lately, and not just to Luke. The Third Division was running into problems. Men were disappearing in the night, and the road had to pay more contractors to bring them back. The convict gang was almost the size of the regular crew. Tensions were high in both camps, and it was all Luke could do to keep the men working some days. John was having the same problems, as were the other contractors. Everyone but Howard. The Celestials didn't complain, bought their own food, and worked hard. When Luke's hunting crews had increased the food, it had contented the men for awhile, but then they wanted more whiskey, and more time off. A group of Mexicans and Irish had taken to picking fights with the Celestials because they were making them look bad. Twice now, Luke had gotten bruised, stopping fights.

*"But tomorrow's another day,"* Luke thought. His breathing slowed; his thoughts grew more quiet. He closed his eyes and finally drifted off to sleep, just as the sky above him was lighting up.

The sharp clang of steel against steel roused Luke from his slumber. Daylight still thick with shadows filtered through the high square window of the bunk car. The scent of chicory and baking bread filled the air. How long had he slept? His eyes scanned the car and found that all of his fellows had dressed and left to begin work. He should feel guilty, but he didn't.

Luke lay with his eyes closed, enjoying the few moments before he started the day. "Clang." Then a pause. "Clang." He could almost hear the hammer swing during the pause. "Clang." Luke had once been on the swinging end of that sledge. He could feel the memory in his muscles, of lifting the hammer, then heaving the weight into an arc that took control of you on the downward side. He waited expectantly for the next chime. His muscles waited for the sudden shudder to run through them when the hammer made contact with the steel spike. Through the effort of muscle, one inch at a time, the spike drove itself into the pinewood tie. Every muscle tensed in Luke's body as it waited for the next chime.

The chime never sounded. "Thud." A scream pierced that same still air. Luke's blanket flew into the air as he headed toward the sound of the scream. The blanket tangled around his legs and he fought to be free of it. He hit the wooden floor running, not even bothering to put on his boots. He wore only his union suit, but nobody even noticed.

Work had stopped throughout the camp as people gathered in a circle, hovering like buzzards around a dying animal.

When Luke reached the center of the circle, he found Francis O'Rourke sitting full on his tail in the dirt. He cradled one hand with the other while his partner, Pat Coughlin, stood by helplessly.

He didn't make a sound, but his face showed the pain he was feeling. Luke knelt on one knee next to the injured man. "Can you talk, Frank? What happened?"

Frank started to open his mouth but the words came out of the other large Irishman's mouth instead. "T'was my fault, Sir," Pat said in his usual thick accent. "Frank's hammer slipped and I couldn't stop me swing in time." Luke looked up and saw the guilt and self-anger on the face of the skinny redhead. He couldn't be sure, but there might be tears in those green eyes. He looked away. That was too personal.

He turned his attention back to Frank. Frank was shaking his head, his lips pursed tightly. "Twasn't . . . 'is . . . fault, Boss," came the slow reply, as he fought against the pain. Luke could see the edge of his hand. Already it was turning purple. Not a good sign. Frank fought for better control, then found it. He took a shuddering breath, and could speak more clearly. "I was just clumsy. Shouldn't of 'ad me 'ands in the way. Tweren't Pat's fault. I'll be right as rain by and by."

Luke reached for the man's hand, to examine it, but Frank didn't want to let it go. Probably didn't want to see it. "You have to let me, Frank. You know you do." He looked into Frank's eyes and willed him to let go. "Someone go get Skel," he ordered. He felt movement as someone left the circle in search of the doc. He never took his eyes from Frank's. Finally, Frank relented and allowed his hand to be withdrawn from where it was protected by his arm.

Luke didn't touch the wounded area. He held Frank by the forearm, supporting the hand, so it could remain untouched. The hammer blow had connected with the fleshy part of Frank's hand, between his thumb and index finger. The index finger was already swollen purple, but the thumb looked okay. The skin was broken and raw where the steel met his hide. "I gotta see if it's broke, Frank."

Frank nodded tersely, but his arm shook. Luke probed the swollen flesh with careful fingers. Frank shook but held still. Small sounds rose from his throat, and most of the men started to move away. It was rude to speculate about the accident in front of the people involved. But later they would. It was human nature.

Skel arrived, wheezing heavily from the burst of activity. He spent a few moments examining the hand. The bones weren't broken, as far as Luke could tell, but he wasn't a doctor. Skel said he wasn't either, but he knew how to do medical things. He could bandage a wound, and, so he said, birth a baby, although he would never be put to the test on this crew. Luke had wondered several times if maybe Skel had been a doctor in a previous life — before the war.

After a few moments of observation, Skel said, "We'll have to lance this. It'll burst if we don't ease off the pressure."

Luke agreed with Skel's diagnosis. Already Frank's finger was twice the size of the one next to it. The skin was purple and swollen around the nail, which was already turning black. He'd lose the nail for sure, but it'd grow back. Luke could see fear in Frank's eyes.

One man had lost a finger to gangrene from lancing, and Frank had shared his tent. He'd watched Dale's finger turn green, then black, right before Skel had to cut it off. It was only Dale's stubbornness about changing the bandages that had caused it, though. Skel should keep the gangrene out with bandages, but they wouldn't help the stress on the skin from the welling blood.

Luke took the bull by the horns. He wouldn't let Frank seal his own fate out of fear. "Want something to bite down on, Frank?" he asked.

A tear squeezed out of the corner of one of Frank's eyes. It left a clean line down his dirty face. "Can't," he said finally. "Me teeth are too bad." He laughed bitterly. "Meant to see a dentist on my last job, but spent the money on a woman instead. I could use a dram of whiskey, though."

Luke nodded. "Skel," he ordered, "Get the man some whiskey when you get your tools."

"Colonel?" Skel asked softly after he had moved off a bit. Luke turned. Skel motioned him over with a movement of his head.

Luke went to the dining car to stand next to Skel. "What's the problem?" he asked quietly.

"We ain't got no whiskey," he said in a whisper. "We're out."

Luke forgot to breathe for a moment. Out of whiskey? With the rough-cut crew of men he was running, that was almost as bad as saying the pay train wouldn't arrive.

"I've been trying to talk to you for a couple of days, Colonel. Truly! I've been watering it down, trying to make it last. Denver swears it's been sent, but it ain't never arrived. We have a trace on it, but that doesn't fill the barrel." Luke nodded numbly. He was beginning to have vague misgivings that they were being sabotaged from inside the company. He'd like to believe it was just coincidence, but if the D&RG

had spies in the Midland camp, who was to say there weren't well-placed saboteurs working on their road?

"I've got some whiskey in the cabinet under my bunk," he said. "Use it all if you have to. I'll talk to the other contractors to see if they can spare some, and then take the wagon to Glenwood for more." Skel nodded.

Li Sung walked up, just as Luke was going to talk to Howard in the tunnel. He bowed low and said, "Honorable Boss, this lowly worker has idea. Maybe help." Skel sniffed in disgust and left Luke to talk to the headman.

"Okay, Li, what's the idea?" Luke glanced toward the tunnel. The rock drills were running hard, but he hadn't heard one of the frequent explosions for some time.

"I overheard your conversation with the cook, Colonel," Li said. "I did not intend to eavesdrop, but I might have a solution."

"Out with it, Li," Luke responded. "We don't have much time." He turned to watch Skel return to Frank's side without a glance toward Luke and Li.

"If you have no whiskey to ease this man's pain," Li continued, "Our opium, what your men call 'dream smoke,' would make him able to bear the procedure. It was what our herbalist used on the worker in the spring."

Luke thought about it, but shook his head. "He won't use it. It might work, but Frank'd never touch anything your men use."

There was a brief flash of something in Li's eyes. Maybe anger, maybe pain. Luke couldn't help either one, and didn't try. "And you would let your man suffer needlessly because he was too proud, or too stubborn, to let our drugs help?"

Luke shrugged. "I'll offer it to him, but don't be surprised if he refuses."

Li nodded curtly.

When Luke returned to the site, Skel was using a match flame to heat the edge of a knife. Luke didn't understand when Skel talked about "germs" and the like, but he really did sound like a medical doctor sometimes.

"God praise you for the whiskey, Colonel. A fine Irish blend," Frank said after taking a long swig.

"Frank, the Celestials have offered a drug that would make you not feel this at all. No pain. But it's your choice." Luke sat back on his heels, waiting for an answer, while Li stood quietly in the background.

Frank watched nervously as Skel finished heating the blade to a bright red. Then he set his jaw. "I'll never touch the dream smoke, Colonel," he said. "I be a God-fearin man. I've heard tales of a man who killed his wife and wee boy while on the Chinee' drug." He took another swig of whiskey. Luke watched Li shake his head sadly and move away.

Luke motioned to two men. "Hold Frank still, so's Skel can do his job. The rest of you, get back to your work." The men nodded, and Frank let them press his shoulders to the ground. He took another long pull of whiskey and then nodded to Skel. The others moved slowly to return to their posts.

While Skel operated, Luke went to find Howard Ballard. He heard a scream echo through the cañon, then another, then the curses of the men as they struggled to hold Frank down. Luke walked to the mouth of the Jackson Tunnel. Inside the confines of the rock, the sound of the drill was incredibly loud. He shook his head until he was accustomed to the sound, then walked inside. They had but 600 feet to go to complete the tunnel. Luke looked around as he walked toward the crew. The ceiling was high enough to permit the tall engines to go through. The picks and shovels of his rock gang had made the floor of the tunnel reasonably even. The rock drill stopped abruptly. The sudden silence startled Luke.

"Howard?" he called. "You up there?"

A string of curses was followed with, "I am, but I wish I weren't."

Luke joined the crew. The men were sweating. The air was thick with smoke. "Are there problems?" he asked, concerned at Howard's attitude.

"Blast that John Morton!" he exclaimed with fervor. "Hanged if he wasn't right. Just look at this!"

Luke looked toward the face of the tunnel. A wide band of hazy white was set into the granite. "Quartz?" he asked.

"Worse!" Howard exclaimed. "It's quartzite." At Luke's questioning look, he explained. "It's prefractured. If we try to blast this, it'll only strengthen it, make it harder to drill. We'll have to try to go around the vein."

Luke's face showed the concern he was feeling. "Is there enough room before the cliff to do it?"

"Danged if I know," Howard said. "I'll have to get Morton in here to see if we can make a second turn in the tunnel without risking the line. If we can't make another turn, well . . ." he said. "We'll have to drill through it without blasting. It'll set us back *months*."

Luke took in the news. "I'll get John right over here to help. Any problem with my crews continuing to level the bench in here and get the rails laid?"

Howard shook his head in annoyance. "Might as well. I'm held up until we can figure this out."

As Luke left the tunnel, the sun was just rising over the edge of the cañon. The day was not starting well. He found John Morton in the caboose, drawing his transit readings in a grade notebook. After explaining the situation, Morton hurried to the tunnel. Luke caught up with David Price and explained the situation. David said he would get his crews to the other side of the tunnel and start to work on grading on the Glenwood Springs side until the tunnel could be completed. As Luke was leaving to go check on O'Rourke's injury, David exclaimed, "Good Lord, Colonel! Look!"

Luke followed the pointing arm. Rising above the cañon rim was a plume of smoke. It grew as they watched. It was already too large for a campfire, and there weren't any Utes in that direction. It could only be one thing! A fire at the mill! Their last hope of bringing in this job on time was going up in smoke! Luke headed toward the pack animals. He quickly grabbed the reins of the nearest mule, and said to David, "Get some men up to the mill." He mounted the large animal, hands taller than his regular mount, and said over his shoulder, "Bring picks and shovels and buckets for water!" Luke spurred the animal into a startled leap and headed back east to catch the road to the mill. The big male raced over the slippery roadbed, sliding this way and that, but always keeping his balance.

"Fire!" David called, and rang the triangle at the dining car. Those men who weren't in the tunnel reached for whatever tools they could find. A train of men soon followed in Luke's path up to the mill.

By the time that Luke reached the sawmill site, the fire was nearly extinguished. The five men who ran the mill were technically part of Luke's rock gang. But they preferred to work alone, so as long as the timbers were cut and the ties reached the job on time, Luke left them to their business. He was mentally berating himself for not checking on them more often as he rode into the blackened ruins.

The foreman of the crew, John Tuttle, met Luke as he arrived.

"What happened here, Tut?" Luke asked, his voice harsh with anger. He didn't need another delay. Couldn't afford one.

"Don't rightly know, Colonel," the man said tiredly. "We've been talkin', tryin to figger it out. We was having breakfast in the main tent. We hadn't even started the saw. Dale heard someone spookin' the stock and we all headed to the corral. Two men on horseback — regular horses, mind you, not mules, was driving off the draft stock. We chased them down for a bit, on foot, but when we came back to get our saddle mounts, the mill was on fire."

"So," Luke thought, "*the sabotage has stepped up a pace. Horse thieving and arson.*" Without the draft horses, they couldn't move the ties to where they worked, but without the mill, there were no ties.

"Then this wasn't an accident," he said, more statement than question. He wrinkled his noise at the smell of burning pine. The air was still thick with acrid smoke. Wisps rose lazily from multiple spots in the clearing.

Tut shook his head quickly. "The fire started in two spots. One started right in the mill house, the other in the storage shed across the way."

The other men arrived to find that they weren't needed. Some men began to shovel dirt onto the smoking timbers. Several walked the edge of the clearing to check for hot spots.

The men looked to Luke, understanding the seriousness of the loss of the mill. He addressed his tired, shaken crew. "We will bring this rail into the station," he said forcefully. "No matter what they do to stop us. We will complete this line. On time, and before the Midland!"

There! It was finally spoken. The whispers around camp were made real by Luke's words. Sabotage. The crew responded with fervor.

Shouts went into the still, smoky air. "Yes, Sir!" "You can count on us, Colonel!" "We'll beat the taffards!" "God bless the Rio Grande!"

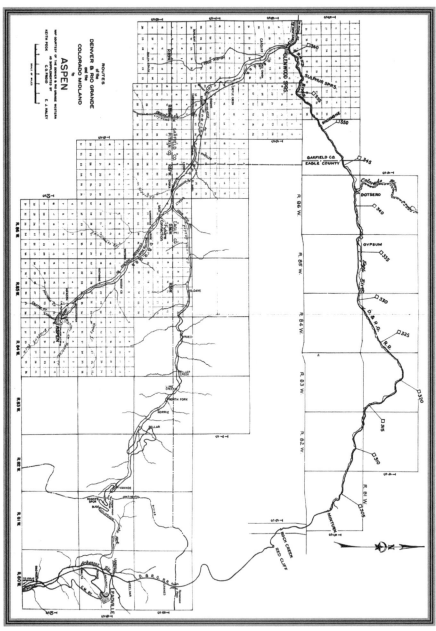

Routes taken
by the two
railroads,
starting at
Leadville.
(Denver
Public
Library
Western
History
Department
and Denver
Westerners,
Inc.)

*David H. Moffat, President of the D&RGRR during the construction. (Rose & Hopkins photo: Denver Public Library Western History Department, #H-123)*

*John A. McMurtrie was the former Chief Engineer for the D&RG during the Palmer Presidency. He left to form his own company and was responsible for track laying on the Glenwood Springs to Aspen line. (Colorado Historical Society, #F3233)*

*This drawing typifies a snowslide covering the tracks of a Colorado rail line.* (Harper's Weekly, Colorado Historical Society, #10029537)

*Tunnel #1. Note the use of rough-hewn local logs for ties.
These ties were likely made at the No Name Creek mill,
which was burned down by the previous owner to protest
the commandeering of the mill by the railroad. (Colorado
Historical Society, #33620)*

*Second Tunnel, taken before the track was completed.*
*(W. H. Jackson photo: Denver Public Library Western History*
*Department, #WHJ-1645)*

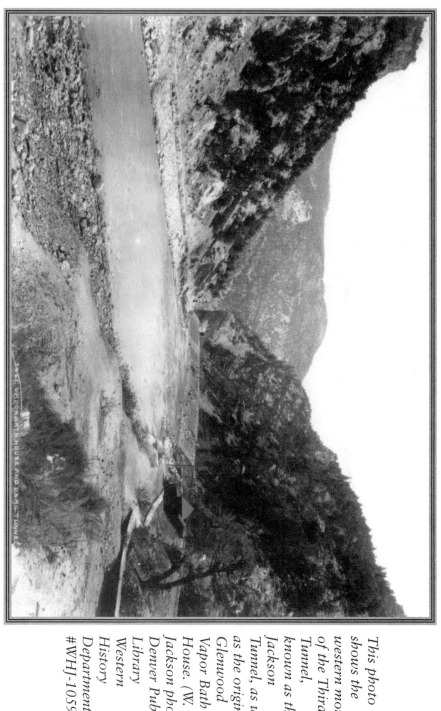

This photo shows the western mouth of the Third Tunnel, known as the Jackson Tunnel, as well as the original Glenwood Vapor Bath House. (W. H. Jackson photo: Denver Public Library Western History Department, #WHJ-1059)

Looking down the Roaring Fork Valley into Glenwood Springs. (Hook photo: Denver Public Library Western History Department, #X-8763)

The beginning of the toll road from Glenwood Springs over Cottonwood Pass. (Detroit Photographic Co. photo: Colorado Historical Society; #WHJ-10294)

*The various stages of track construction are evident in this exceptional photo taken near Woody Creek. Aspen is in the distance. (Denver Public Library Western History Department, #WHJ-607)*

A typical tourist excursion of the time, similar to those that occurred during construction. Note that the third rail to handle standard gauge trains had been added by the D&RG. (Poley photo: Denver Public Library Western History Department, #P-1667)

The railyard at Aspen at the grand opening of the Aspen line. (Denver Public Library Western History Department, #Z-206)

These two engines were assigned to the contractors by the D&RG to build the railroad. Some of the construction management and their families are pictured. (McClure photo: Denver Public Library Western History Department, #MCC-3178)

This narrow gauge locomotive was used by the D&RG Western (Palmer's company in Utah) during the same period. It can be viewed at the Colorado Railroad Museum, Golden, CO. (Cathy Clamp: photo)

A typical narrow gauge passenger car. It can be viewed at the Colorado Railroad Museum, Golden, CO. (Cathy Clamp: photo)

*General Palmer spared no expense to make passengers comfortable, as is evidenced by this plush narrow gauge car. (Cathy Clamp: photo)*

*Below: Tight quarters were the rule in the narrow gauge world. Economy of space allowed for four bunks, a pot bellied stove, cabinets and a writing desk. (Cathy Clamp: photo)*

# The Ute Chief

## GLENWOOD SPRINGS, COLORADO, SPECIAL EDITION, 1887

PRICE, 10 CENTS

The Ute Chief was the predecessor to The Glenwood Post, and was the weekly newspaper for the Glenwood Springs Region that followed the progress of railroad construction. The following are excerpts from actual newspaper articles written at the time. The full articles can be viewed either by contacting The Glenwood Post or on microfilm at the Colorado History Museum Library.

### July 9, 1887
### Over the Cliff.

At about four o'clock last Sunday morning Michael Murray, one of the men employed at the east end of the Rio Grande tunnel, while on his way to begin his day's labors fell off the cliff and was lost in the Grand river. Murray had been drinking the night before and is supposed to have been in a befuddled condition at the time of his fatal mishap. Murray had started out on the trail which leads from this end of the tunnel to the upper end around the rocky cliff. At the starting point there are numerous false trails in the way of ledges of rock which run up the face of the cliff and soon pinch out to the sheer face of the wall. Murray is supposed to have reached such a point and was crowded into the flowing river below. No trace of the body has been found. Murray was a man of about fifty-five years of age, 5 feet 7 inches in height, of compact build and florid face, smooth shaved. He was formerly a drayman in New York city and is supposed to leave a family whose residence is said to be on 21st street, in that city.

### July 9, 1887
### A Roaring Fork Victim.

On Tuesday evening last James McNulty, who was in the employ of Kyner & Co., the D. & R. G. contractors, at a camp six miles up the river, stripped off his clothing and took a plunge into the Roaring Fork. He was seen by his companions swimming, with skill and executing various maneuvers, till finally he passed into a riffle and was suddenly lost from view and has not since been seen. It is the same story of drownings in the mountain streams. The excessively cold temperature of the water is supposed to cramp its victims. McNulty was 24 years of age and a native of New Jersey. He was commonly known as "Shorty" among his companions. Contractor Kyner ordered strict search to be made, but no trace of the body has yet been found.

### July 9, 1887

An exchange has learned that there are just 1,100 unmarried men in Garfield County against 26 maidens fair. We believe that these figures lie . . .

### July 20, 1887
### The D. & R. G. Tunnel.

The 1350 feet tunnel on the D. & R. G. extension from Leadville to Glenwood Springs is more than half completed. Both Captain Ballard and Mr. Rundell, the contractors on the work, put the date of its completion at September first at the latest . . . The compressed air drills are doing good work and some days remarkable progress is made. They are under cover now 850 feet which leaves but 500 to be completed . . .

### July 30, 1887
### D. & R. G. Tunnel and Track.

The D. & R. G. railroad is in reality but 16 miles from Glenwood Springs if we run the measuring tape right up the canon. More than this, the last word down from active operations tells us that the end of the track will be at Delta creek, a distance of only 13 miles to-night . . . The contractors on this work, Ballard, Rundell & Co. are making fine progress and believe this work will be done shortly after the first of September. There is a piece of rough and rocky grade just above this which may make a trifle longer delay. So from this we conclude that the "Baby" road will reach us and be ready for general business from the first to the twentieth of October.

### September 17, 1887
### DAYLIGHT.

Messrs. H. C. Ballard & Co., contractors on the Jackson tunnel, have for the past few weeks experienced considerable trouble in driving the head on account of the bad air, and for that reason have been compelled to let the

Ute Chief *excerpts.*

"bench" stand and push forward work on the heading. At the present writing there are but thirteen feet to open the head, and a hole is being drilled through so that wire can be connected . . .

#### September 17, 1887
### The Midland is Coming.

Advice from Frying Pan are to the effect that track laying on the Midland down that stream is progressing at a remarkable lively rate. It is claimed that a construction train will be a the mouth of that stream, on the Roaring Fork by the first of next week . . .

#### September 24, 1887
### THE TUNNEL.

At the present time all interest in this section is centered upon the Jackson tunnel, just above the town. Bets are being made upon the time of its completion . . . its completion will mark a new era in the history of Northwestern Colorado . . . A little over eleven miles above Glenwood Springs, or a mile and a quarter above Cottonwood Falls, is the first tunnel, which is designated by the company as No. 1. This tunnel is 280 feet in length, and is driven through red granite. No. 2 tunnel is located about a quarter of a mile above Cottonwood Falls, or a little over ten miles from town. This bore was driven a distance of 133 feet through the blue granite, and is pronounced the finest tunnel in the country . . . The Jackson tunnel is 16x22 feet in the clear, with an arched roof. The total length is 1331 feet . . . This company got ready for the work in hand before operations were commenced. One of the finest pieces of machinery ever used in the state for that class of work was secured, consisting of the necessary power, two large Norwalk air compressors and eight Sargent drills . . . The character of the rock driven through has principally been quartzite, and of late has been very hard to work . . . During this entire month the average driving per day was a little over two feet--about two and a quarter. Over 400 feet of tunnel was driven by hand.

#### September 24, 1887.
### President Moffat Responds.

The following telegram . . . has been received by the committee appointed to correspond with the officials of the Rio Grande. "Your dispatch received. Considerable work still remains to be done before the Glenwood Springs line will be ready for general business. I think I may say, however, that a party composed of some of the company officials and perhaps a few guests will leave here on Monday, October 3rd, reaching Glenwood Springs on Tuesday, the 4th. I am obligated to you for the courteous invitation contained in your telegram, and desire to assure the people of Glenwood Springs, through you, that it shall be the aim of the company to build up the material interests of their city, and to work in harmony with them for the prosperity of our state . D. H. Moffat, President"

#### October 8, 1887
### HERE AT LAST

It did not seem possible that the road could be completed in so short a time, and it was even thought by some that it would not come at all . . . The snow had not entirely disappeared, the ground was frozen and the work at first necessarily very slow. But the "Little Giant", never known to be daunted, kept on emitting the rock, and the ranchmen of the Eagle River valley were soon awakened by the shrill whistle of the locomotive . . . The mouth of the Eagle was finally reached, a distance of forty-three miles from Red Cliff, and it was only eighteen miles from Glenwood Springs, but that distance was to be made in one of the most rugged and precipitous canons in Colorado-- the Grand Canon of the Grand. It called forth all the skill and ingenuity of the company to blaze a track through it, and they planned to beat all their previous records in mountain railroad building. Solid cliffs that towered thousands of feet above the bed of the river were there to be shot down; in places they seemed to defy the construction of a road, and the company were satisfied to blast out only half their road bed; over 1,700 feet of tunnels were to be driven, and in places it was impossible to get or set machinery . . . They did not reach the City on October 1st, but it was so G--da-- awful close that it did not interfere in any manner with the welcome accorded to them on Wednesday evening last.

#### The Banquet.

A banquet was spread at 10 o'clock at the Hotel Glenwood, of which our guests and the representative people of the county sat down to, the party not breaking up until a late hour.

#### Notes on the Event.

The public did not get through celebrating until Saturday morning, as a "Celebration BBQ" was given last evening. The banks were closed in the afternoon, businesses were generally decorated, and all classes joined in the celebration. Enough giant powder was exploded to drive another tunnel. Late in the morning the last reports were heard from this high explosive. The illuminating committee did an excellent work. The transparencies were pleasing to the visiting brethren, and the city was one blaze of light.

#### October 8, 1887
### Shooting Affray.

A shooting affray occurred . . . which at first promised to be serious. But little is known of the matter save that Jack Carney, a railroad man, shot a saloon keeper named Joe Bart. Bart was shot in the forehead, the bullet coming out of the side of his head. To avoid mob violence, Carney was taken to Aspen for safe keeping.

Ute Chief *excerpts*.

## THE TELEGRAMS.

Following are some of the many telegrams sent between the construction crews of the D. & R. G. and contractors and the management of the railroad in Denver, Leadville and other stations along the way. The majority of the actual telegrams identified in the article, "To Aspen and Beyond" by Jackson Thode, L.M., are in private collections and estates and were unavailable for this edition. The telegrams herein are from the collection of the Colorado Railroad Museum, Golden, Colorado.

> Denver 9/27
>
> S P King
> GS                    1245 pm
>
> Three 3 Bunk & Two
> 2 Dining Cars from
> The Second division
> Two 2 Bunk Cars from
> Gunnison and one
> from Lathrop and
> one 1 from Burnham
> were shipped to you
> yesterday and two 2
> or Three 3 more will
> be shipped from the
> 4th Div, within a few days.
>                    R E Briggs

NOTE: These cars still hadn't arrived by October 19th.

*Telegrams*

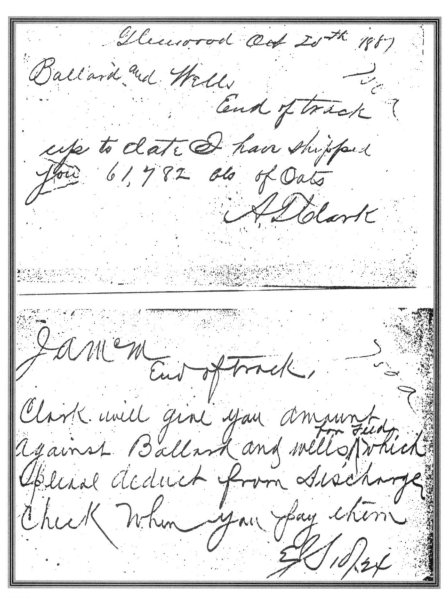

*Telegrams*

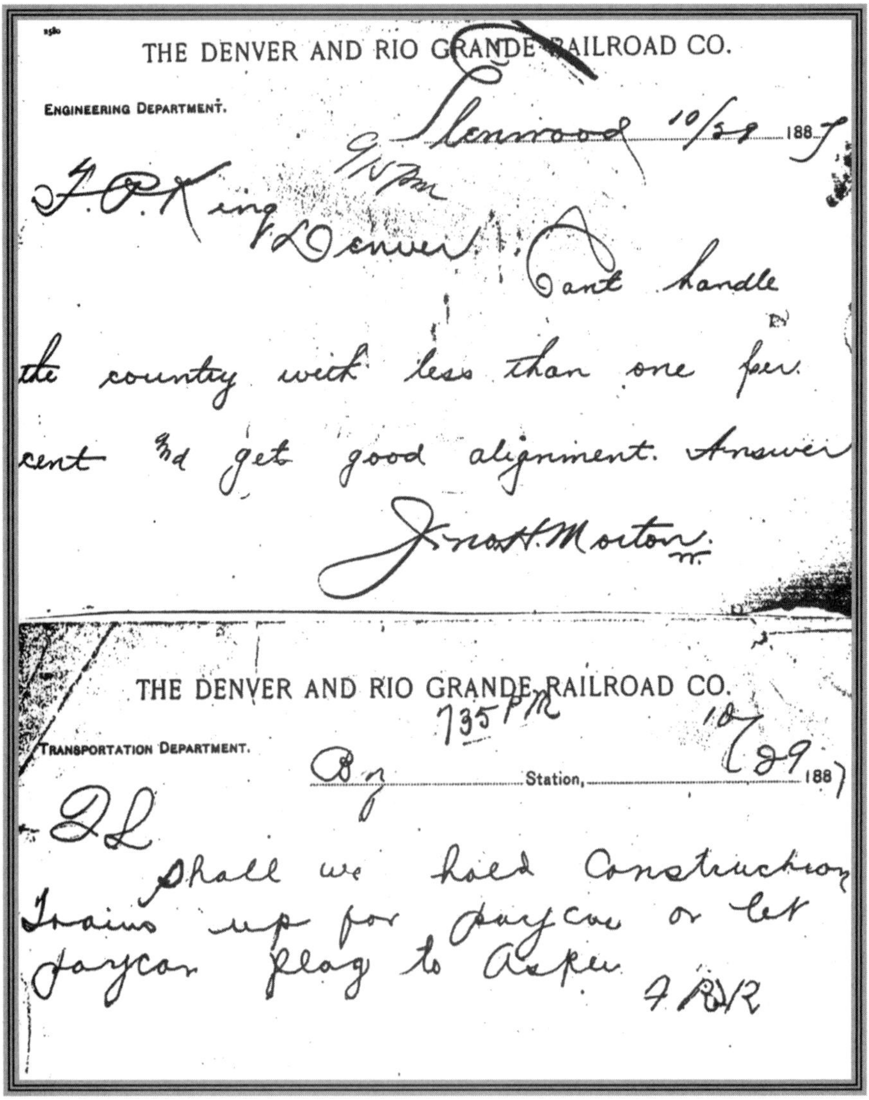

THE DENVER AND RIO GRANDE RAILROAD CO.

ENGINEERING DEPARTMENT.

Glenwood 10/28 1887

9/10 pm

J. P. King, Denver: Cant handle the country with less than one per cent and get good alignment. Answer

Jno H. Morton W.

THE DENVER AND RIO GRANDE RAILROAD CO.

TRANSPORTATION DEPARTMENT.

735 PM

By Station, 10/29 1887

DL

Shall we hold Construction Trains up for paycar or let paycar flag to Aspen. FRR

*Telegrams*

*Approach to first tunnel Grand River. (W. H. Jackson photo: Denver Public Library Western History Department, #WHJ-96)*

*Showing bridge from D&RG Depot. (Denver Public Library Western History Department, #8836)*

Entrance to the Cañon of the Grand River. (W. H. Jackson photo: Denver Public Library Western History Department, #WHJ-399)

Trans RR
D&RG
contruction track
Colorado River
Cañon near
Glenwood
Springs. (George
Beam photo:
Colorado
Historical
Society,
#1002938)

# CHAPTER 17

As Luke rode into the Third Division camp, he tried to think how to tell his fellows the bad news. Not only would they have to begin to haul ties, and risk yet more delays, but John Morton had concluded that there was no room in the mountainside for another turn. H.C. Ballard & Company would now have to drill through the layer of quartzite without blasting.

Luke's spirits were low as he arrived at the command tent. Ricker looked up briefly from his desk, where he was writing correspondence. His eyes narrowed and he laid down his pen. He leaned back in his chair, crossing his arms over his chest. "I'm growing concerned by your bearing, Colonel."

"As you should. We've trouble in the Second," Luke replied. It was best to speak frankly and then spend time planning how to manage the problems.

"Sit, then, and tell me the situation. Should I pour coffee or whiskey?" Ricker asked, surprisingly calm. He waited near the table for a response.

"If it were later in the day, I would say whiskey," Luke said tiredly. He removed his hat and sat down. He rubbed his forehead briefly. When he opened his eyes, a glass nearly half full with whiskey sat in front of him. He looked at Ricker with surprise.

"I'm in charge of this project, so if I say it is later in the day, then it is." Ricker nearly smiled, again surprising Luke. Luke noted that although Ricker held a cup of coffee, it smelled suspiciously of the same liquid as in Luke's glass. His eyes were heavy lidded and bloodshot.

Luke explained about the mill and the delay in the tunnel. Ricker asked questions and nodded at times. Luke continued to be amazed at how calm he was.

Luke was finishing another sip of whiskey when John McMurtrie walked into the tent. He started when he saw Luke and Ricker talking, a half-empty bottle between them.

"Come in, John," Ricker said, with an odd edge to his voice. "Sit down and have a drink with us." McMurtrie took off his hat and walked toward the pair with a suspicious expression.

Ricker pushed the bottle toward John, and leaned backward to grab another glass from the rack.

As McMurtrie poured, Ricker said, "Colonel Ballister was just regaling me with tales of woe from the Second." There was something in Ricker's voice that raised Luke's hackles. It belied his calm manner. Was he having some sort of mental collapse?

As Ricker's breathing grew shallow and his eyes began to shine brightly, Luke suddenly understood. The man was holding onto his control by his fingernails.

"May I ask what the difficulties are?" John asked. Luke brought him up to date. He spoke slowly and chose his words with care.

"You're taking this quite well, Colonel Ricker," John said, with a glance at Luke.

Ricker stood and walked to his desk. "Fortunately, gentlemen, I anticipated this problem." The announcement brought startled looks from both John and Luke. This seemed to amuse Ricker. "Although I know you will both be loathe to admit it — occasionally, I do earn my pay."

Ricker pulled sheets of paper from his desk and walked back to the table where the pair sat.

"I expected the tunnels to cause us problems." He handed John and Luke a sheet of paper, covered with figures and names. His mood seemed to darken. "Colonel, you will spend your time during the delay concentrating on running the telegraph line through to Glenwood." His face then began a startling transformation. Barely controlled rage lay under the calm words. He held one finger aloft. "I don't care if Ballard has to drill one single six inch hole through that last five hundred feet!" Ricker's voice was harsh. "But I will have the line to our station by September. The cost of the continuing Western Union billings is unacceptable! They're throwing off our budget."

Luke and John sat, open-mouthed at the abrupt change in manner. Ricker continued his tirade, oblivious to the looks on their faces. "Once the line is run to Glenwood, you will reassign the telegraph gang to the Third Division, so we can proceed to run the lines to the Satank and Emma stations. We may then at least *correspond* without delay."

Ricker's next words were calm, but his features were distorted, his face flushed. "While I had hoped to return to Denver to attend to my other duties, I believe it is in the best interest of the road that I remain here to oversee the construction."

In a moment, his entire face changed again. His eyes grew cold and hard and burned with a black hatred. His voice dropped by several notes. "Make no mistake, gentlemen, my opinion of you both has not changed. I do not like you, nor do I trust you."

Luke and John froze. They couldn't be sure of Ricker's next actions, but they both tensed, watching him closely. His face reddened and his jaws clenched tight. His breathing grew fast and shallow. "But, I had no say in your hiring. You are who I have been given, and it is with you that I must work, blast it!"

He stood and walked to the stove and started to pour coffee in his cup. He stopped abruptly, then threw the tin cup into a wooden print rack, where it bounced with a loud clatter. John looked at Luke with raised brows, took a large gulp of whiskey and waited.

Ricker whirled around and pointed one shaking finger at them. His other fist clenched until it was white. "I will be watching you both! If this spur is not completed on time; if either of you fail me in this, I *guarantee* that you will never again work for this road, nor any other that I can influence!"

Suddenly, he smiled at them, a baring of teeth on his reddened, angry face. The flashing eyes and angry countenance were dark and foreboding. "Now, Mr. McMurtrie, if you will fetch Mr. Boyd, who is running the Carlisle group, and the other road foremen, we will make our plans to increase production."

# CHAPTER 18

Luke had jumped at the opportunity to ride out of camp and deliver the telegrams to town. He needed some time alone to think. The strains of this project had taken their toll on all of the men, but it was Ricker who worried Luke the most. Try as he might, Luke couldn't think of a blasted thing to do about it. The meeting with the heads of the gangs and the contractors had gone badly. By the end of the meeting, Ricker was screaming at the men about lost production and throwing glassware. Veins had bulged in his neck. Once or twice he'd been barely able to breathe. Luke could only hope that once the rails arrived in Glenwood, he would take to his railcar office with his staff and remain there.

Luke took a deep breath and shut his eyes. The porch swing moved under him gently. Just a moment longer and he would mount up and head back to the Second.

"Thought I'd find you here," said a familiar voice. Luke opened his eyes. John was leaning on the gate to the Johnson house. "Get those telegrams sent?"

"I did," Luke replied. "I was just resting Star a bit before I headed back to the Second."

John reached over the fence and opened the gate latch. "I'd heard that about you," he said with a note of friendly teasing.

"Heard what?" Luke asked. A tight knot formed in his stomach.

John looked up onto the porch, and said with raised brows. "That you had the best rested mount in the whole of the division."

"What are you saying, John?" Luke began with annoyance. Then the front door opened and Maribelle stepped out. She was holding two small plates. Her eyes squinted as she tried to recognize the newcomer.

"Hello," she said politely. "Can I help you?"

Luke made introductions. "Miss Maribelle, this is John McMurtrie. He owns the company that's putting in the tracks to Aspen. John, Miss Maribelle Johnson."

Maribelle's face brightened and she smiled. "Oh! I'm very pleased to meet you, Mr. McMurtrie. Luke has told me so much about you."

John raised his brows. He tipped his hat politely, and said with a sly smile, "A pleasure, Miss Johnson. I do hope that *Luke* has been kind in his statements." Luke winced at his tone.

Maribelle laughed lightly. John noted how Luke's face lit up at the sound. "Most assuredly, Mr. McMurtrie. Luke has the greatest respect for you, and has been singing your praises."

"A good thing to know, Miss." He noted the plates that Maribelle was holding. "I'm sorry to interrupt, but I'm afraid I've come to fetch *Luke* back to the front."

Maribelle looked at the plates. Her face fell. "Oh, dear," she said. "I had hoped you could join us for a moment. My father's been abed for some time, so I made his favorite treat — iced cream with fresh strawberries. We're famous for our strawberries here in Glenwood Springs. But he's feeling too poorly right now, and I hate to see it go to waste. I had asked Luke to share some with me. Do you have just a few minutes, Mr. McMurtrie? I would be quite distressed to have it spoil." She gave her most winning smile. John looked at the plate longingly and bit his lip. How many months had it been since he'd had such a treat?

He looked at Luke, who was grinning at him. John cleared his throat, and said, "It would be a shame to see all that effort go to waste."

"My very thoughts," Luke said. "Surely whatever problem has been imagined by Colonel Ricker can wait five minutes."

"It might take me that long to find you," John commented reasonably as he reached for a plate. "After all, you'd already headed to the Second."

"That I had," Luke said with twinkling eyes. They both took a bite of the dessert just as Maribelle disappeared into the house to fetch a third plate for herself.

They didn't dally. Soon they were riding companionably back to the site. The verdant landscape moved by them as they trotted their mules up the valley. Although the time at Miss Maribelle's had been pleasant, John's inference continued to bother Luke. He decided to be direct.

"John, about your comment earlier — are you accusing me of laying down on the job?" He tried to keep his voice mild, but a hint of anger peeked through.

John sighed and tipped back his hat. He set the reins on the saddle and looked at Luke. His mule could pick the way through the rocky terrain without his assistance. "Nobody can accuse you of not working, Luke. Even *Ricker* can't find fault with your performance, try as he might. You do the work of four men each day. Everybody knows it. But *I* know you better. You're capable of more than you're giving right now. You're distracted, and it's obvious why. It's clear Miss Maribelle has set her sights on you. All I'm saying is — either dance with the girl or leave her to the next partner. Put your mind back on the business at hand."

Luke started. The knot began to form in his gut again. "It's not that sort of relationship, John! She's a sweet girl, but she's a *child*!"

"She's marriageable age, isn't she?" John replied. "She can keep a house and such?"

Luke furrowed his brow. "Well, yes, of course. She can cook and do fancy work and other womanly things." Luke gave a small smile as he thought about her. "She's right smart about world events, and keeps a fine house. She is a bit clumsy, but she'll do someone proud as a wife some day."

It took a few moments, but eventually the underlying question sunk in. "Surely you're not suggesting that *I* . . . ." The words were startled, nearly panicked.

John had nodded when Luke mentioned "clumsy." He had been watching the other man as he spoke, and took a moment to lessen the tension. "You have noticed that the girl's nearly blind, haven't you?"

"Maribelle?" Luke asked, his brow furrowing. "Blind? No. She can see just fine."

The sounds of metal against stone greeted their ears. Voices in the distance were growing louder. John shook his head. "I've a sister with poor vision, Luke. The signs are all there. Squinting to see things at a distance, tripping over small objects that she should have noticed. No, I think if you were to check with her folks, you'd find that her sight is very poor, indeed."

"As to the other, Luke," John continued, noticing Al Clark approaching on his mount. "What you feel for the girl is none of my concern, but her feelings for you are plain on her face. So, I'll say it again — dance with her or leave the floor." He put spurs to his mule and moved to meet Al at a slow lope.

Luke mused about John's statements as he led Star along the riverbank. Loud laughter and calling was coming from a group of men ahead of him. He saw Frank Kyner head toward the group, and decided to investigate the commotion.

A group of five men stood on the bank of the river, calling to another man who had removed his outer garments and was frolicking in the water.

Frank walked up to the group and asked one of the men, "Thomas, what goes on here?"

"Shorty was just showing off his swimming skills. He's quite good. Watch him!"

Frank shook his head with annoyance. "Dang fool. I told him that the water's too fast here to swim." He looked at Luke. "He's one of my men. Says he grew up in New Jersey, and there's no water as difficult to swim as the waves on those shores. He told me that the other four people who drowned this year in the Roaring Fork were simply *unprepared*." He shook his head again. He cupped his hands around his mouth. "McNulty! Come out of there!"

"Just cooling off, Boss," Shorty replied. Luke watched as one of the men tossed a coin to the swimmer. He dove head first into the chilly water and retrieved it as the men laughed. Luke raised his brows. He was quite good.

"Do that somersault trick again, Shorty!" another man called out.

He received a thumbs up and Shorty dove again. This time, he didn't reappear. The men waited with anticipation, but after many seconds passed, they grew concerned. Thomas called out to him, "Shorty! Quit foolin' around. Show yourself!"

Frank and Luke headed for the water at a run. Frank watched the shores for any sign of his man. Thomas and the others continued to shout his name, frozen where they stood. Luke removed his boots and stepped into the water. Shorty might have gotten a foot or hand caught between rocks under the waves. Luke walked until he was up to his knees. He could feel the undercurrent tugging at his legs. The fast moving water dragged him downstream as he tried to reach the spot where Shorty had gone under. His foot slipped on a moss-covered rock underfoot, and he submerged to his neck. He gasped as the icy water closed around him, numbing his skin. The river caught him and he started to move. He tried to regain his footing, but the current was too swift.

"Luke!" Frank called. Luke turned his head to see Kyner holding onto John McMurtrie's arm a hundred feet downstream. His hand reached out, hoping to grab Luke as he passed. Struggling against the flow, Luke kicked and paddled toward the bank. It was a futile effort. The water tumbled him like a toy. He was already chilled to the bone, and it was an effort just to take a breath. He began to shiver almost uncontrollably, and his stomach muscles started cramping.

The current slammed him against a large rock. When his head hit stone, he saw stars and nearly passed out. Pulled under the waves, he came up spitting water. A sharp pain erupted in his side as another rock slammed into him. Then, he was jerked to an abrupt halt. A hand held his shirt, but the river was not ready to give up its prey. It continued to pull against him.

"Heave now, boys!" came John's rich baritone. Luke felt the fabric of his shirt start to tear. He tried to force his legs to push at the riverbed, desperate to help his rescuers with the fight. It was no use.

They were numb and nearly lifeless. How could the water be so blasted cold in July?

Still, somehow they managed to wrest him free. Soon he was on the bank, gasping and coughing up dirty water. Frank, pants wet to the thigh, pounded on Luke's back to help him to clear his lungs.

"You alright, Luke?" John asked. "Thought we'd lost you, too."

"Couldn't find your man, Frank," Luke said, shivering and coughing. Words were hard to form through his numb lips. "I'm sorry."

"You were a fool to make the attempt!" Kyner snapped. "Shorty was probably already drowned when you went in."

Luke looked at him with flashing eyes. "I had to try. We lost a man in the Grand on Sunday because nobody tried to save him!"

Kyner shook his head sadly, then began to bark orders to his men. "Thomas, get some people and head downstream. See if you can find Shorty."

"What if we only find his body?" Thomas asked sadly.

Frank's jaw set. "Then bring him home. We'll give him a proper burial. It's the very least we can do." The men nodded and began to walk the river edge.

It was an exhausted, bedraggled Luke that appeared before Ricker. "Most people remove their clothing before swimming, Colonel," Ricker remarked snidely.

Luke had expected such a comment, and only shook his head with mild annoyance. John gaped at Ricker incredulously. "Colonel Ballister just jumped into a river to try to save a man from drowning."

Ricker's brows raised. "And did he save him?"

"Unfortunately, no," Luke said. "I wasn't able to find him."

"Then you shouldn't have jumped in," Ricker said dismissively. He changed the subject without another word. "Where are the tracks at this point, Colonel?"

Luke sat down. His legs were still unsteady and his chest hurt from the swallowed water. The pain in his ribs was a constant ache. They burned when he coughed.

Ricker strode forward angrily, hands clasped behind his back. "Did I give you permission to sit down, Colonel?"

Luke looked up at him with narrowed eyes. "I didn't ask. Nor do I intend to." He watched Ricker's face redden. Ricker opened his mouth to speak, but Luke cut him off. "The tracks are laid to the east side of Delta Creek. I have already made plans to split the rock gang into three groups."

"I believe — " Ricker began, but Luke raised his voice and spoke over the words. He was tired of worrying about Ricker's mental condition. He was annoyed with himself for his own inattention, annoyed with Ricker for making each step a struggle, and determined to take back control of the project.

"I intend to place one third of the rock gang with the telegraph gang. The faster the poles are set, the sooner the line will be run to Glenwood. The second gang will be assigned as additional labor for the Carlisle group. I expect to reach Gypsum by the first week of August, and be through to the third tunnel by September. The third gang — " began Luke, but this time, Ricker cut him off.

"The third gang will be sent here to the Third to help with excavation and bridge building."

Luke's eyes narrowed and he stood. He was inches taller than Ricker, so he looked down on him when he had stepped to within a few inches of him. His words were a barely controlled yell. "No, the final third will be added to the surfacing gang, so that we have a ready, complete track available to bring the train into the Glenwood station."

McMurtrie watched the contest of wills closely. He knew this confrontation would determine how the rest of the job was managed.

Luke's eyes went cold and he stared into Ricker's face. Each of the next words was clipped, carefully enunciated. "I was given a specific task by the president of this road. That assignment was to increase production and ensure that the lines would reach Aspen before the Midland, *without fail*. While I appreciate that you are the general superintendent, Colonel Ricker, I intend to accomplish the task set before me in the manner *I* feel most appropriate. Do we understand each other?"

When he spoke again, Ricker's voice had dropped several notes and his words were dark and dangerous. "I will have your *job*, Colonel Ballister."

Luke lowered his voice as well. "You would be welcome to it, Sir!" He straightened up to his full height. Even with his torn shirt dripping muddy water on the floor of the tent, Luke was a commanding presence. "But I believe that you are ill-prepared to lead the men in both divisions, and the goal must continue to be beating the Midland to Aspen." Each syllable dripped contempt. "Therefore, I will *strive* to set aside my dislike of you, and will work toward the best interests of the road. If you are *unable* to do the same, then I suggest you consider returning to Denver early and leaving us to the task." He turned on his heel and left the tent.

John caught up with Luke as he was mounting Star. "You've made an enemy, Luke. Do you really feel that's wise at this juncture?"

"Ricker was my enemy long before this expansion, and will continue to be after," Luke said strongly. Star pranced impatiently, tossing her head in the quickening breeze. "You were correct, John. I haven't been paying proper attention to my job. I intend to change that."

John nodded his head in approval. Luke wheeled the mule around and took off at a gallop out of the Third. It was time to return to his post.

# CHAPTER 19

By the fifteenth of August, only three hundred feet remained in the tunnel. Ballard's crew struggled to drill through the ever-widening layer of quartzite. Luke spent long days pushing the crews in the First and Second Divisions. The rails had reached Gypsum, and the telegraph gang was just to the east at Delta Creek. With the extra help of the rock gang, they were setting as many as twelve poles a day, and stringing line on four. Luke had split the work days into three shifts of eight hours instead of two shifts of twelve. The extra free time seemed to calm his troops. Twenty more men had been added to the pay rolls a week before.

"Know what I miss most, being on the gang?" a worker asked his fellow outside the bunk car where Luke sat writing a status report to Colonel Ricker. Luke tried not to listen so he could concentrate on the figures in front of him. "Set ten poles yesterday," he wrote. He shook his arm to regain feeling. The ribs wounded in the river were slowly healing, but if he sat for long periods, his arm went numb.

"What's that?" the other man asked.

The hammer swung again, and a chime reached Luke's ears, "Sitting on the porch watching my two boys cranking ice cream. My woman, she'd add fresh peaches from the tree in back."

"Got a pair of girls myself," the second man said.

Luke shook his head, fighting to remove the image of his last taste of ice cream from his mind.

Each day it was more difficult to keep his mind on work. The strangest things would remind Luke of Maribelle's soft voice and demure manner. "Just passed Delta Creek," he scribbled. "No hay again today. Lost one burro and two more have fallen ill. Have arranged to graze stock on local land in exchange for future transportation. Received eight cars of iron instead of requested ten. Will put trace on your shipment of grain."

He picked up the paper and blew on the ink. Then he folded the message and handed it to the courier. Colonel Ricker was demanding daily status reports. He had arranged for a man to arrive each mid-day to collect the missive. Luke closed the blotter book with an annoyed shake of his head.

There was no point complaining about the unnecessary repetition of work. Moffat had assumed the presidency from Jackson, and had taken to Ricker as a comrade. Luke sighed, and swung down from the bunk car to fetch Star and head east to check on the progress of the telegraph gang.

"Colonel!" Howard Ballard called, "A moment?"

"What can I do for you, Howard?" Luke asked as he threw a saddle over Star's back.

Howard took off his hat and wiped his brow with a shirt sleeve. "I know you've had your men working east of here, but I will soon need them to return to remove the bench inside the tunnel."

"The header's nearly complete, then?" Luke asked. "I thought you had another few hundred feet to drill."

"The quartzite is thinning, and we're nearly back to granite." Howard was obviously pleased. "My lieutenant, Mr. Gunn, reports the vein has all but disappeared from the western face. I believe we can return to our earlier progress. The men are preparing now to blast and see if we can open the header again. If so, I hope to be done by the first week of September."

Luke nodded his head. "Excellent. Let me take a look at your progress. I *would* like to get the telegraph gang a bit further before I remove the extra men, but if it appears you're ready for them, I can put them back in the tunnel with you."

Howard nodded. Luke followed him to the mouth of the tunnel. Ballard stopped to listen a moment at the tunnel entrance. "Odd," he said to Luke. "I thought they would be readying the powder."

Luke listened as well. "I can hear the compressor, but no drilling. Think we should check on them?"

Howard nodded, and the two entered the tunnel. Darkness closed around them, cool and still. Their footsteps bounced off the high stone ceiling, echoing into the distance. The deep blue-grey granite faded into black as they walked further into the mountain. It took a few minutes for Luke's eyes to grow accustomed to the dim cavern.

"David?" Howard called. "Is all well?" There was no reply.

"Captain Hanford?" Luke shouted. The two men hurried forward.

The air tasted dusty and stale in Luke's mouth. As they reached the tunnel bend, Luke felt his chest tighten. He was growing short of breath. Howard appeared to be having difficulty breathing as well, and pressed a hand to the rock wall to avoid falling. A lantern on the ground near the header was flickering violently. There wasn't enough light to see clearly, but there was no sign of movement where the crew should be.

By the time they reached the header face, Luke was feeling dizzy and nauseous. He looked at Howard, just in time to see the other man drop forward and lay still. Luke turned in slow motion back to the header. There was no oxygen here, deep inside the mountain. Grey spots ate at his vision, and he dropped to his knees. Twelve men stretched before him on the ground. He had to get out of the tunnel! Had to get help!

He labored back to his feet and stumbled to the first fallen man, Edward. He appeared to have been carrying Captain Hanford when he collapsed. He put fingers to the Irishman's neck. He wasn't breathing, and his pulse was faint enough that Luke knew he would soon die if he didn't get air. Moving as fast as he was able, he checked each man. Only one man was in worse shape than Edward, and was significantly lighter than the big redhead. When he turned the man over, he realized it was the worker whose face had been injured by powder in the spring. He put hands under the man's arms and began to drag him. The effort was almost too much.

Again and again, he pulled and stumbled. His starving lungs burned. Sweat painted his brow and ran down his face in rivulets. His feet felt like lead. The weight of his charge was almost unbearable. The muscles in his shoulders screamed with effort. He was on his knees more often than his feet by the time he could see the bright circle of daylight. But it was still too far. He wouldn't make it.

"Help!" he called weakly, hoping someone would hear. He collapsed to his side. Each breath was agony, but he held onto consciousness, calling with every rasping intake of stale air. It was only when he heard footsteps in the rubble and saw shadowy figures rushing toward him that he allowed the darkness to claim him.

Luke woke on his bunk. He felt for all the world like a mule had kicked him. His head throbbed. Every muscle ached. He hoped everybody had survived. He tried to sit up, but his body refused to obey. His exhaustion was so complete that all he could do was let the velvety blackness settle over him.

It was hours later when John McMurtrie entered the rail car to check on Luke's condition. He was still feeling poorly, but could at least keep his eyes open without his head pounding. John sat down on the bench next to him, watching him with concern.

"Did everyone make it out?" Luke asked. His exit had been so slow that he feared the worst.

John nodded. "Thanks to you. It was touch and go with several of the workers. The big redhead is in about the same shape as you. The others are all up and walking around. Captain Hanford is proclaiming you a hero for saving him and his men." John shook his head. He tried to lighten the moment by saying, "You're simply determined to let this job be the death of you, aren't you?"

Luke forced a weak smile. "What brings you to the Second, John? Not that I'm not pleased to see you."

McMurtrie winced. "I hesitate to add to your misery, Luke."

Luke's head resumed its pounding. He closed his eyes and brought up an arm to put over his face. "Just tell me. How much worse could it get?"

John sighed and removed a folded sheet of paper from his shirt pocket. "I delivered this in person so I could josh you, but you've taken all the joy from it." He handed the paper to Luke, who eyed it warily.

The evening light was growing dim inside the bunk car. Luke turned the paper at an angle to catch a small shaft of light from the high glass window. He read the familiar handwriting of Colonel Ricker:

> LRB: Please identify location of "Maribelle Creek" in today's report. Cannot locate on my maps. Respond by Mr. McMurtrie. RER

"What in blazes?" Luke's eyes widened. He swept the blanket from his body, and sat up swiftly, to his regret. John watched him with concern.

The pounding in Luke's temples worsened as he forced himself to stand. Thankfully, it was only a single step to reach the small writing desk. He sat down heavily and lifted the black padded lid. Trembling fingers turned the delicate onionskin paper to his last entry. He could only stare numbly at the words, written in his own hand.

"Delta Creek," he whispered, more to himself than John. "It's Delta Creek where the lines have been strung to."

John nodded quietly. "I know, Luke."

He looked at John, but couldn't meet his friend's eyes. There was a stabbing pain in his chest that had little to do with his ribs.

"I'm a trifle tired," he said shakily, continuing to stare at the words on the page. "Could I be alone to get some rest?"

"Surely," John said, rising. "I'll be heading back to the Third. I'll think of something to tell Ricker." He walked past Luke, and briefly put a solid hand on his friend's slumped shoulder. Without another word, he stepped from the car.

# CHAPTER 20

Edward awoke with a start. Frantic eyes looked around until he realized he was in his tent. Had it been a dream? He moved his arms and legs, and took a deep breath. Muscles ached. His chest burned with each breath.

He had been in the tunnel with the others. The final hole had been drilled. They were ready to add the blasting powder. First, one lantern went out. Then the next began to flicker. One by one their headlamps had gone out. One of the Chinamen took off his hat and shook the miner's light, muttering in the Chinee' language. Then he just dropped to the rock floor.

Others sank to their knees. One held his throat as though he couldn't breathe. It was then that Edward realized the air had gone bad. He picked up the nearest man, Captain Hanford, to carry him out. After that, he remembered nothing.

"You awake yet?" asked a voice from outside.

"Aye," he said, then coughed violently. His throat was as dry as dust.

Tommy's friend, Skel, entered. Edward knew he was an able physician so he allowed himself to be examined.

"You're not too much the worse for wear," Skel said. "You're blasted lucky to be alive. If it weren't for the Colonel and that Chinaman . . . ."

Edward's eyes narrowed. "What Chinaman?" he asked suspiciously. He was not surprised to find that Colonel Ballister had once again helped him.

"Why, the one what shares your tent," Skel said with a note of surprise. "Dragged you out first thing — before his own men! Didn't think he had it in him. Stronger'n he looks. Beat on your chest to start your breathin'."

Skel put the shiny reflector and other tools back in his black bag. "Looks like you'll heal. Captain Hanford said to tell you you'll be paid full wages today. Colonel Ballister told him you were trying to bring him out when you collapsed. Right grateful, he was. He'll probably stop by later."

Edward lay on the bed for long moments after the doctor left. He was annoyed with himself for not having been able to withstand the bad air long enough to save the others. He'd grown weak, in part because he was still fretting about Tommy, God rest the boy's soul. Edward hadn't had the heart to write Katie about the misfortune. What could he say to ease the loss of her son? Nor had he told his family of his new wages and duties. That would mean he would have to tell them who he worked with. To say that he owed a Chinaman for his life! Would his wife even lay beside him again? Still, he reasoned, *"the man is actually a Brit."* Then he winced.

Oof! That was hardly better!

As well as he got on with Li — sharing stories of the Isles and sporting contests, he missed his fellows on the rock gang. They hadn't spoken to him since he joined Captain Ballard's crew. While they'd never say it to his face, he knew what was in their thoughts. He should work with his own kind. He'd tried to explain he must support his sister now too, but they hadn't heard. Edward sighed. Lord, how he missed their company — the drinking bouts, and games of chance.

And yet, why should he be deprived of all games? They hadn't planned a contest of any sort since the new management arrived. Colonel Ballister seemed a reasonable man, he might allow summat. Edward had not tested his mettle against the others since the last spring. Before the winter winds set in, they should have some games. Perhaps horse riding, or — yes! A game of hurling! How long had it been since he'd held a beloved cam-n? How long since he'd run down field against the opposition to score a goal? Surely they'd allow a wee bit of sport one sunny afternoon.

# CHAPTER 21

"*It seemed such a good idea at the time.*" Luke pulled his aching body from bed. The morning had arrived far too early. Still, it was his own blamed fault. When Edward had approached him, more than a month ago, about planning a contest, he'd dismissed the idea.

Then, when the second week of September had come and gone, and the tunnel was still not complete, he reconsidered. The rock gang was restless. There was nothing for them to do. Even the telegraph gang was waiting for Ballard to finish drilling a hole in the header to allow the lines to get through. David Price's crew was waiting for air to be restored to the tunnel so they could lower the bench and grade. Luke was not the only man with time on his hands. Restless and bored, the men had turned to gambling and drinking, both morning and night. Even Luke found himself drinking too much. If and when the tunnel was ready, they'd be in no condition to work.

Reluctantly, he'd approached Edward and suggested that perhaps a game would be wise. It was Luke's hope it would prevent more of the desertions occurring in the night. It also might take his mind off his own troubles. With the assistance of some of Luke's rock gang, Edward had found a location for a hurling field, a game Luke had never heard of.

"Never heard of hurling?" Edward exclaimed as he stared at Luke, aghast. "Why, Sir, it's the finest game in all the world! The Gaelic Athletic Association has published rules, and there are organized matches all over the Isles!" He shook his head sadly at Luke's ignorance and muttered as he walked away, "Never heard of hurling! Poor soul!"

The camp electrified at the idea of a contest. The Irish quickly formed a team, the Americans another. The rules seemed simple, but the "hurley sticks" had to be constructed from pine logs. The Irish crew spent long hours cutting and smoothing the sticks.

"They should be ash," muttered one man to Edward with an annoyed shake of his head.

"And do you see any ash trees in this cañon, Jacob O'Toole?" Edward snapped. "Praise the Lord that we may even play! Would the fiend Carpenter have allowed it?"

"Aye," spoke another man, whittling on a nearly completed hurley stick. "Edward speaks true. We should be thankful we've the opportunity. And be doubly thankful that John Reilly saw the new rules posted by the GAA. He's written them down for all to see."

"Published just this last February," Reilly told Edward, "in *United Ireland*. I'm not fond of Rule Nine, but I suppose it's for the best."

That night, Edward asked Li to read the rules to him. "Number Nine," Li said, "No player to catch, trip, or push from behind. Penalty, disqualification to the offender, and free puck to the opposite side," he said. The two men looked at each other in surprise.

"That certainly takes the sport from it," Li said in his thick, British accent. Edward had smiled.

The next morning, Edward presented a completed cam-n, or hurley stick in English, to Colonel Ballister.

Luke turned it over in his hands and shook his head at the strange contraption. It was nearly three feet long with a round handle and flat curved paddle. Edward explained that the concave cup in the stick was used to move a small ball from one end of the field to the other. It was passed in the air from stick to stick, or hit along the ground to reach the goal.

"Not much of a sport," Luke said with a shrug.

"Not much of a sport!" Edward exclaimed. "There are twenty-one strong fellows on each side." He gave a sly wink. "The sticks occasionally find other uses than handling the ball . . . ."

Luke's brows raised appreciatively. Well, that was a different matter!

The Irish had invited Luke to join their team. He was flattered. Still, it wouldn't look good to choose sides. Instead, he offered to be an official. He had dutifully studied his copy of the rules after both sides agreed to his serving as referee.

Luke stepped gingerly down from the bunk car. He had a limp, his ribs hurt, and his mouth was swollen almost shut. Skel passed by, racing from tent to tent.

"I've only time to tend open wounds and broken bones, Colonel! I've lunch to prepare, after all!" He hurried to his next patient, tsking and muttering with each step.

Luke shook his head at his own foolishness. He was fortunate to have only bruises, scrapes, and cuts. Others hadn't fared as well. Hurling was no sport — it was an armed riot! Two on the American team had broken arms, and one Irishman was unconscious from a stick to the head. Others bore long gashes in legs and ribs, or sported black eyes from leaping ditches and dodging trees. Luke wouldn't be surprised if a tooth or two remained on the field.

He should have insisted that Rule Nine remain, even though both sides requested it be removed. He shook his head as he wandered the camp, hearing the moans and groans of the workers. Yet, even as man after man had been carried from the field, others readily took their place. In the end, the Irish had won, seven goals to three. Side bets had been rampant, and it was finally decided that the winners were to receive the losers' allotment of whiskey for the night. The Irish were up into the wee hours, cheering and singing in their native tongue.

Luke looked up to see Howard Ballard and Philip Filius racing toward him. "We're through!" Howard exclaimed. "We've an air hole in the rock, and it's all granite between!"

Luke tried to smile, but his jaw was too tender from getting in the way of an overhead clash. "How long until you'll need the crews?"

Howard and Philip looked at each other, panic plain on their faces. "We need them now!"

"We're a little worse for wear after the game yesterday, Howard. I had considered letting the men sleep in for a bit."

Howard's eyes went wide and he grabbed Luke's shirt, grasping it with both fists. Luke reared back in defense and Ballard immediately dropped his hands with embarrassment. "There's no time, Colonel! It's already the seventeenth of September! We must reach Glenwood by October first!"

"The first, or even the third hardly matters. We've plenty of time to reach Aspen before the Midland."

Howard was nearly beside himself. Mr. Filius mirrored his partner.

"Is there something you're not telling me?" Luke asked.

Ballard threw up his hands. "It's that blasted contract, Colonel! We *must* have rails into Glenwood by October first!"

"Why?" Luke asked.

"We forfeit our entire fee." Philip Filius spoke quietly, bending close to Luke so no one would hear. "It's the same with all of the contractors," he confirmed. "There's a clause that says that if tracks capable of carrying a fully loaded train do not reach the depot in Glenwood by October first, we all forfeit our pay.[2] Carlisle's company stands to lose nearly two million if we don't get there. Garrison Carlisle is ready to have a mental collapse!"

Howard continued with quiet hysteria, "Our company will go bankrupt, Colonel! We've mortgaged our lives to bring in the rock drills for this job."

Luke stared openmouthed at the pair. "Why would you sign such a document?" he asked incredulously.

"Jackson and Moffat wanted speed and were willing to pay the price. They hired the best, and agreed to whatever we bid," Howard said.

"Except," Philip said, "for the October first clause. It didn't seem a problem in April, as we only had the one tunnel. We saw no difficulty completing by the deadline."

"We can make it, Colonel, but we need your help! We've but thirteen feet to drill to open the header. There's air a'plenty now. If we use dump carts on each end, I believe we can finish the job on schedule."

Luke sighed. It was certainly not his fault that the contractors had signed such an imprudent contract, yet he was certain Colonel Ricker would find ways to fault him if he delayed. "We'll get started immediately," he told the pair with another sigh. The relief on their faces was evident.

"Are you sure you want to do this, Colonel?" Skel asked minutes later. He gaped at the bruises that blossomed all over Luke's torso. Newer black and purple marks blended with the fading yellows and greens. Luke knew what they looked like, but he had no choice. He nodded and Skel began to wrap a cotton bandage around him.

"I've five men down with broken bones. They'll be useless with a pick or shovel," Luke replied. He gasped as the strip of cloth tightened. White dots filled his vision for a moment. "We need every man available to lower the bench."

Skel intentionally tugged the bandage to elicit another gasp from his patient. "If you believe you're in better shape than the others, you're sadly mistaken, Colonel."

Luke turned to the doctor and said coldly. "Just bandage the ribs, Skel. I'll be fine once I'm trussed."

Skel shook his head, and tied off the bandage. "You'll be fine once you've spent a week in a relaxative sanitarium, Colonel, but not until."

"We've barely time to sleep, Skel, if we expect to get road to Aspen on time."

Skel nodded. "I do understand, Colonel," he said quietly, "but if you injure those ribs one more time, I can't guarantee that you won't do permanent damage. You could puncture a lung."

Luke was taking short, shallow breaths against the tightness of the cloth that bound him. At least his chest no longer burned. The pain had dulled to a mild throb. He could think of no response to Skel's concern, so he simply stood and gingerly walked toward the mouth of the tunnel where shovels and picks were already ringing against the stone bench.

Skel shook his head tiredly and returned to the dining car to begin breakfast for the third shift.

Howard assigned Edward to work with Luke's rock gang. Getting the bench cleared was paramount. Every hand was needed. Edward watched Colonel Ballister with growing concern. The man was strong, but Edward could see him wince with pain with each shovel thrust.

Luke had early on abandoned all hope of swinging a pick. Even working the shovel was difficult. He wasn't sure whether the little assistance he could provide was even helping, but he had to try. The constant, numbing pain kept him from thinking about the decision he'd made. He knew what he had to do when he reached Glenwood and the welcoming party. He'd known since he'd received her letter by post, written on paper that smelled of sweet perfume.

When the shift ended, Luke collapsed into an almost drugged sleep. He desperately needed to check on supplies, but simply couldn't walk the distance to the corral. In truth, he doubted he could even mount up. He promised himself he'd take care of it, after just a short rest.

He woke with a start to see sunlight streaming in the small window above. Had he slept until daybreak? John Morton was just entering the car as Luke struggled to get his shirt on.

John shook his head as he watched Luke's effort. "Why don't you stay down today, Luke?" he asked. "Deal with paperwork if you must, but don't go back into the tunnel."

"I don't have the luxury of resting, John," Luke said as he grabbed onto the table to lower himself to his bunk where he could put on his boots.

"And yet you allow it for others," John said.

Luke looked up at him with a face full of self-anger. "It's my fault they're injured, John. If I hadn't agreed to the hurling match, we would have a full crew. As it stands, it will take every man working extra shifts to finish the bench, grading, and tracks in time."

John sighed. "If you are determined to destroy your health, then at least allow me to assist with the correspondence and paperwork to bring in the supplies."

Luke closed his eyes. He felt as though a huge weight lifted from his chest. "If you could do that, John, it would be heartily appreciated! I haven't had the time to even see if we have the ties and rails to *complete* the line once the tunnel is graded," he admitted, allowing a hint of his exhaustion to show.

"I believe we have the rails to do it, and I'll do the calculations now to determine the number of ties needed." Morton grinned wickedly. "Then I'll double the order!"

Luke laughed, then coughed from the sharp pain. "I've yet to receive word about the depot," Luke said. "I've asked for a crew of four good men to build it, but I haven't found where the materials disappeared to. If you could contact the Pueblo yard, maybe we can hurry it along. Colonel Ricker says they've got the new agent, DeRemer, ready to be installed, but nowhere to put him."

"I'll check into it," John nodded. "I know we're down to one car of coal. I'll wire for another three so there's no delay in getting all the way to the Glenwood yard."

It was a blessed relief not to have to worry about the paperwork. Morton was a good and able man. Knowing that part of the job was in capable hands allowed Luke to focus his attention elsewhere. Shift after shift slipped by Luke in a blur of painful effort. Those with broken bones had watched the gang boss take their place in the rocks, and found tasks they could perform to help. One man with a broken leg propped himself against the tunnel wall and received rocks to place in the cart. Men with broken arms placed strong backs against the carts, pushing them to the dump area.

Ballast was smashed and placed over the ties. The operation worked as an oiled machine. Cheers and hurrahs of the crew filled the air when the tracks reached the western edge of the tunnel and started down the grade to Glenwood Springs.

Curious townspeople came to watch. They mostly stayed out of the way — all except for Ernie Douglas, that pesky reporter from the *Ute Chief*. For months now, he had shown up without notice and wandered around the site, asking questions and generally distracting the crew. Moffat insisted that denying the press access could harm public relations. Howard seemed the least annoyed by the man, so Luke let him deal with answering the man's never-ending string of questions.

Not nearly enough ties had arrived, nor had the batteries for the telegraph, and Luke had sent several terse cables to Leadville to determine the delay.

They were only a few hundred yards from Glenwood on October first. The owners of the contracting companies had quietly gotten drunk. So goddamned awful close! They decided to fight the road if they refused to pay. It was, after all, the ties not arriving that prevented the progress, not their work.

"We'll take it to the Supreme Court if they fight us!" Gary Carlisle exclaimed during the drinking bout. "The grade is done. That was the deal!"

"And so's the tunnel!" Howard exclaimed strongly, pounding a fist on the table of the bunk car. He pointed at Luke. "It's *your* people at fault!"

Luke gave no argument. They were right. "I'll tell Moffat the truth," Luke said with a shrug. "The ties didn't arrive. Whether it will have any effect, I can't say."

"Just look at it," David Price said with glowing happiness. The others stood and peered out the windows with him. The little town of Glenwood Springs stretched before them tantalizingly, just a few yards away. "Isn't it beautiful?" The men all nodded, problems forgotten for at least the night.

# CHAPTER 22

"Glenwood Springs Welcomes the Denver & Rio Grande!" exclaimed the banner stretched across Grand Avenue from the bank to the dry goods store. The entire town had turned out for the celebration as the rails finally reached the Glenwood yard. The materials for the depot still had not arrived, but there was plenty of time to get the building done before the Aspen line was completed.

Jarrod Talbot was one of the guests on the excursion train which included President Moffat's private car, "The Maid of Erin." He beamed as Moffatt shook hands with Luke and congratulated him on a fine job. Ricker had arrived and retired to his Special without a single word to Luke, although he glared when Moffat shook Luke's hand. He had not yet been seen at the festivities.

Moffat, however, was so jovial that Luke tentatively brought up the issue of the contractors. They hovered nervously here and there, afraid to approach the president of the road.

"Not to worry, Colonel!" Moffat boomed affably. Luke winced in pain as Moffat clapped him on the shoulder sharply. "I'm not an unreasonable man. If the delays were ours, then of course we'll honor the contracts." Luke could see Garrison Carlisle grin as he casually walked by in the background.

Moffatt then asked about the line to Aspen. "When will you begin the next leg of construction?"

Luke sighed. As much as he would like to give the men a well-deserved rest, he knew they had to continue on with building. However, he had heard much grumbling that the men were not able to partake of the efforts of the town's welcoming committee. The residents had gone to a great deal of trouble to illuminate the town with lanterns and prepare barbequed ribs and beefsteaks for the guests and crew. Whiskey flowed like water. Another sudden blast sounded from the hillside. Enough blasting powder was being exploded to drill another tunnel!

Luke grasped Moffat's arm lightly and moved him to the side a bit. "I admit I'm afraid of the state the men are in," he said quietly. Moffat immediately sobered. "In April we had discussed offering a pay raise when we reached Glenwood."

Moffat's expression darkened. His words held an edge of terseness. "As you can imagine, Colonel, money is especially scarce right now. Is there any way to avoid such an expense?"

Luke shook his head. "I'm afraid not. We need every man available for the task. There's the same distance from here to Aspen as from Gypsum to here, and it's uphill the entire way. Even with the efforts of the Third Division, there's at lot to do. Reports have it that the Midland is within sight of the town of Frying Pan.[3] That puts them nearly ten miles ahead of us."

The news brought a startled look to Moffat. His manner changed abruptly. "Of course then, Colonel! You may use whatever resources you need to complete the line before the Midland. If additional pay will keep the men, then pay them! But please use discretion, Colonel. I'd hate to arrive in Aspen only to bankrupt the road."

The interview ended when Quimby Lamplaugh strode up with Governor Adams. "This is a great day for Colorado, Mr. Moffat," the Governor exclaimed as Luke stepped back, blending into the crowd.

He was walking with Jarrod when he first spotted Maribelle. She was devastatingly beautiful in a deep burgundy gown with matching hat. Her hair had been put up, and small ringlets fell around her face. She appeared much older than her nineteen years. Luke had decided on his course while working in the tunnel, and had discussed it with Jarrod earlier. Jarrod had readily agreed.

"Luke!" Maribelle called, her hand waving over the crowd. Luke and Jarrod walked toward her. Jarrod looked at Luke in surprise. "She's lovely!" he said. Luke nodded, and tried to ignore the painful feeling in his chest that had nothing to do with his ribs. Still, it should be done, for everyone's benefit.

"I'm so pleased to see you, Luke," Maribelle said happily. "I hoped you received the letter I posted."

"I did indeed, Miss Maribelle," Luke said. He pulled Jarrod forward nervously and continued. "Maribelle, I'd like to introduce you to Jarrod Talbot. He's one of the paymasters of the road. Been with the company for more than ten years! Jarrod, Miss Maribelle Johnson."

Maribelle held out her hand. "A great pleasure to meet you, Mr. Talbot," she said politely, "Congratulations on your success today."

"An honor, Miss Maribelle," he said, and swept into a deep bow, kissing her hand. She seemed startled, but merely raised her eyebrows and withdrew her hand after a moment.

Luke spoke quickly, before he lost his nerve. "Miss Maribelle, I know you're at a prime age for marrying." Maribelle beamed at him and cocked her head prettily.

"Jarrod's been telling me he's interested in settling down with a good woman and starting a family. He's a fine man, with a good salary and pension. I think he'd be well suited to you."

Maribelle stared, open-mouthed at Luke's words. Her eyes moved from one to the other, then she stared at the ground for a moment while she thought of what to say. When she looked up again, her narrowed blue eyes had darkened to the color of storm clouds. She crossed her arms over her chest, the small purse she carried swinging wildly from her arm.

"If you were interested in discontinuing our courtship, *Colonel Ballister,* you need merely have told me! I understand from the newspaper that there are over 1,100 eligible bachelors in the county, and merely twenty-six women. No offense, Mr. Talbot, but I can assure you I am fully capable of locating suitors by myself! *Good day,* Gentlemen!!"

She spun on her heel and pushed her way through the crowd at a controlled run. After a moment, she turned back to them, opened her mouth to speak, then just made an exasperated sound like a small scream. She threw up her hands and stormed off again.

Jarrod turned to Luke with a look of wonder. "You didn't mention *you* were courting her, Luke. You're a braver man than I! But I'd not worry about her affections any more. You'll be lucky if she ever speaks to you again!"

He hooted with laughter and forcibly shook Luke's hand. "I do thank you, however, for the best entertainment I've had today!"

Luke was more confused than ever before in his life. Why would his good deed have sparked such a reaction? He watched her retreating form and shook his head. He didn't understand women at all!

He moved through the crowd numbly, wincing as men pounded him on the back or shoulder. He went to the tables set up by the committee women, but the smell of the cooking steak made him nauseous.

"Luke!" called a voice from the other side of a crowd. "Glad I found you!" He looked up to see John McMurtrie heading his way at a fast trot. He was pleased to see him. The look on John's face guaranteed Luke distraction from his current dilemma.

"What's the trouble, John?" he asked, almost eagerly.

"There's a brawl over at the bar! It's your man, Jack Carney, again." John pulled on Luke's arm, but let go after he saw the pain on his face. "Ribs still hurting you?"

"Working on the rock gang didn't heal them up much," he said as they headed toward the saloon.

They reached the Silver Nugget just as a shot rang out. It coincided with another round of blasting powder, so most of the townsfolk never even noticed. The pair moved to either side of the swinging doors. Luke pulled his Dragoon, and John produced a small derringer from a holster on his leg. Luke peeked over the door. Men stood around in a circle. The saloonkeep, Joe Bart, lay face down on the floor, the side of his head a bloody ruin.

Luke watched as Jack Carney sat down heavily into a chair. He couldn't stop staring at the body. John and Luke entered the saloon. John took away the man's Smith & Wesson, while Luke pulled him roughly to his feet. John turned over the body. There was a neat hole in the center of his forehead.

Carney looked at Luke as though he didn't recognize him. "I didn't mean to!" he exclaimed. "He made me so blasted angry! It just sort of *happened* . . . ."

Luke held Carney while John went for the sheriff. He returned with Deputy Martindale, who arrested Carney after hearing an account of the fight between the two men. Carney didn't resist at all when the handcuffs were placed on his wrists. He looked at them with blank, lost eyes, and kept repeating that he didn't mean to do it.

"You'd better post extra guards, Deputy!" exclaimed a man from the back of the room. The Deputy turned and tried to identify the speaker. "'Cause we're going to see that railroad man swing for this!" The other patrons echoed the sentiment with shouts and oaths.

"Justice will be done," Martindale said strongly, "but not at the hands of a lynch mob. We've judges and a court to handle this. I don't want to, but understand now that I'll put down any man who tries to take one of my prisoners!"

"Justice?" exclaimed a heavy-set man at the bar. "You mean justice like Mike Ryan got in the spring? That scurvy murderer, Harry Burrows, is walking around a free man today. District Attorney Butcher couldn't prosecute a hole in the ground!" The man stepped toward Martindale. "Joe Bart was our friend and fellow. We'll not see his killer go free!"

Luke could sense a growing tension in the crowd. He started to draw his sidearm again, but Martindale pushed his arm down. "They won't attack us, Colonel. But they've given me notice! I'll have to keep Carney somewhere other than the town jail. It's murder, so we'll have to move him to another county if we hope to get a fair trial. I'll contact Aspen by wire right away."

Luke and John accompanied the Deputy to the jail and secured Carney in a cell. The excitement had momentarily made Luke forget about Maribelle and he strove to continue the trend. Although it had gone as badly as it possibly could have, at least she wouldn't be expecting something he couldn't give.

John and Luke rounded up the crews. They were sullen and angry at first, but quieted when Luke told them he had received Moffat's approval to increase the pay. Their shouts echoed those of the citizens of Glenwood. "We'll get you there, Colonel! Don't you worry!" exclaimed one worker. By the time the sun set, Luke and the crews were back at work. The celebration by management would go on for hours yet at the Hotel Glenwood, but there were still miles to level and grade before Luke could celebrate.

# CHAPTER 23

"The delays in reports have all been in the uptown office,[4] where all business was done until today," John wrote at Luke's dictation. His right arm was useless. Skel had bound it to his body to let the shoulder and ribs heal.

"Mr. Parker did not receive authority to cut in office for Mr. DeRemer and Boarding train until last night. Finished them 10 a.m. today," Luke concluded. John finished the report and handed it to Al Clark to run into Glenwood.

"That should keep Ricker off our backs for another day," John growled "It's hardly our fault Western Union is so backed up with messages that his was delayed. I'll be thankful when our telegraph line is ready for service."

"At least he's staying on his rail car at Glenwood," Luke said with relief.

"I heard he's moving even further east," John said. He stretched, then stood. "Maybe even Gypsum or Leadville."

Luke stood as well. Moving was awkward with his arm bound, but Skel insisted that the ribs would heal better. Luke had finally allowed John to pin up his empty sleeve this evening, to keep it from catching on things.

John preceded Luke from the bunk car. He had deliberately set the boarding step under the bottom stair so Luke wouldn't hop down in the darkness.

"What's the status on the depot?" Luke asked. He was unable to ride in this condition. It was just one more frustration. Still, Skel told him he would probably have use of the arm in another few days.

John laughed. "Typical road efficiency! We've received the shingles, frames, and lumber, but no nails! I've sent Al to borrow a barrel from the dry goods. We'll replace them later."

Luke just shook his head and sighed. "At least we can proceed. What about the iron cars from Chicago?"

"You mean the ones I wired for on September thirtieth?" John asked, anger evident on his face. "Still no sign. It's been nine days! We're fortunate there's some steel at Gypsum and Pueblo or we'd be halted entirely. I *swear* the UP is involved in the disappearance!"

Luke pursed his lips in thought, then shook his head. "If there was *any* evidence of that, John, you can bet Moffat would have them in court!" McMurtrie acknowledged the truth in Luke's words with a nod of his head.

"Still," Luke said, "I doubt they are taking extraordinary efforts to trace the shipment. It's difficult to depend on your *competition* to help you succeed!"

John closed his eyes and shook his head.

The morning of October eleventh arrived with leaden skies that spoke of rain rather than snow. Luke was surprised at how warm it still was in the valley. He had been told that was normal. According to Al Clark, they may not see a snow until Thanksgiving.

Luke had finally convinced Skel to unbind his arm, but Skel was firm in telling him not to over stress it. "Strain it at all and I'll be binding it up once more!" he had said.

Luke mounted Star for the first time in over a week. It felt good to be moving. He wasn't good at sitting still. Now he could help get messages sent to Gypsum and Leadville. Poor Al Clark had been run ragged racing to Glenwood with the ever-growing list of missing supplies. In desperation, John had decided Al would be of more use staying in Glenwood to coordinate the receipt of supplies. Luke was not alone in thinking that if the Midland reached Aspen before them, it would be the D&RG's own blamed fault.

The tracks were laid all the way to Emma now and work was progressing steadily. Luke decided to travel down to check on the progress of the spur into Carbondale. If the weather permitted tomorrow, he might head up to Basalt to check on the Midland's progress.

He passed the bridge gang, hard at work strengthening the piers on one of the trestles over the Roaring Fork. The sharp whistle of a bullet ricocheting off a rock near Luke made him leap off Star and head for cover. The bark of a report, less than a second later, gave Luke some sense of how far away the shooter must be. It was quiet for a moment. "*Could just be a wild shot,*" he thought, but then another bullet hit a nearby boulder, sending a small shower of pebbles over him.

"Get your men under cover, Chapman!" Luke ordered. Men rushed behind large rocks. One slid down the embankment to take cover behind one of the bridge pillars.

Luke poked his head into the open and tried to determine the location of their assailant. A third shot tore splinters of wood from one of the piers, but it revealed the shooter with a small puff of smoke. He was on the bluff overhead. He didn't appear to be aiming at the men, but that could quickly change.

Luke slipped around the rock where he lay, and skirted the edge of the construction, staying in the shadows. It was many minutes, and several rifle shots later, before he snuck up behind the aggressor.

"Drop your weapon!" Luke commanded. He cocked the hammer on his Colt audibly so there was no mistaking his intention. The man tossed his rifle to the side and turned with hands raised. "I wasn't trying to hit no one," he said.

"Kick it to me." Luke spoke with cold calm. He didn't see a holster, but the man could still be armed. His opponent complied. When the rifle was well away from the assailant, Luke called down the hill. "It's okay, Chapman! Your men can come out now. I've got the shooter!" He watched as men moved slowly into the open. When Luke waved his left hand in the air, Chapman responded in kind and started the men to work again.

"I own that piece of land over there," the shooter said, pointing into the sun. "These blamed tracks have let my neighbor's cattle get into my corn! I won't be able to market the grain if the cattle eat it all. I can't rightly shoot the cattle."

Luke looked at him dubiously. "So you'd rather shoot a group of *men*?"

The man looked at Luke stubbornly. "I told you, I wasn't aiming at no one. I just wanted to make my point."

"You'd make it better if you'd simply file a complaint with the road," Luke said, shaking his head. He motioned with his gun. "Let's go."

"Where ya taking me?" the farmer asked. He turned, moving slowly away from Luke, careful not to make any sudden actions. Luke picked up the rifle, trying not to let the other man see the effort it took to bend.

"You have a mount nearby?" Luke asked, motioning the man forward. "We're heading to the command front. You can file a written complaint. If you're damaged by the construction, we'll make it good. We're not out to destroy your livelihood."

As they neared the camp, Luke heard an engine whistle behind him. He turned, hoping to see Engine 403 bringing them the iron cars from Chicago. There was only a days' worth of steel left at the Glenwood yard. They needed more soon. As the train passed, Luke stared. Eleven, no, thirteen passenger cars! No equipment cars, no stock cars, just passenger cars! Were they sending him more men? If so, where would they sleep?

By the time Luke and his charge arrived at the front in Satank an hour later, the entire camp was in an uproar. Ladies with parasols strolled with gentlemen in bowlers. Children laughed and ran along the newly-graded bed. His men, outnumbered more than three to one, leaned on shovels and stared, open-mouthed at the spectacle. There was no hope of laying tracks through the throng of people!

Luke pointed the farmer to the command tent, and quickly rode up to the window of the locomotive. "What goes on here?" he called over the roar of the engine.

"Excursion Extra," said the engineer, named Dugan.

"WHAT?" Luke exclaimed in disbelief. "Have they taken leave of their senses? This is a construction site! How are we supposed to build tracks with these . . . these. . . ," he struggled to come up with a term that could be said with ladies present, "*tourists*, standing about?"

Dugan shrugged. "I only drive the train, Colonel. The Extra was personally approved by Mr. Hooper, the general agent in Denver."

John strode up, also angry. "What in blazes is going on, Luke?"

"The danged fools flagged through an excursion, clear to Satank!"

John's incredulous look matched his own. Luke threw his hands in the air, causing another sharp pain in his shoulder. He shook his head as he grabbed Star's reins. "John, talk with that farmer I sent to the command tent. He's got a claim against the road for lost crops. We have got to get those cattle guards up!" John nodded, grateful to have at least one thing he could accomplish amidst the confusion.

Luke's attention was caught by a group of tourists peering up at a cut in the mountainside. A woman removed a pair of opera glasses from a tiny purse and stared at a massive boulder the men had been struggling to move. It loomed over the heads of the excursionists. Pry rods were still jammed in the dirt beneath the huge rock. Luke's workers had moved an appropriate distance away during the delay, but the tourists didn't appear at all concerned when a dusting of pebbles showered them. If that stone let loose . . . .

Another group was just exiting his own bunk car! Luke wanted to scream!

"For the sake of heaven, John, make sure they don't get themselves killed!" Luke turned to see a group of workers nudging each other and making crude gestures as a decidedly feminine form walked by. "And keep a sharp eye on the men. Let them know they are not to make any inappropriate comments to the ladies. I'm going to take this up with Ricker *in person!*"

"They'll probably beat you back there," John said with frustration.

"*Oh, no, they won't!*" thought Luke. He spurred Star and took off for Glenwood at a full gallop. His faithful mule was lathered and panting by the time they reached Glenwood, just moments before the excursion returned. It was nearly dark when he crossed the yard. He opened the door of Ricker's Special without bothering to knock.

"What is the meaning of sending a trainload of excursionists to the front, Colonel?" Luke asked, breathing hard. The ride to Glenwood had not done his injury any good. Each breath was an agony.

"I have no idea what you're saying, Colonel," Ricker said with annoyance as he looked up from his correspondence. "Mind your tone and tell me your concern."

Luke did. Ricker's brows raised higher and higher as the story unfolded. The whistle of the excursion train sounded as it arrived in Glenwood and Ricker stepped outside with Luke to view the spectacle from the platform on the back of his rail car office. "Thirteen cars?" he asked in astonishment. Luke had not mentioned the number. "That idiot Hooper sent nearly *500* people to my construction front? Is he insane?"

He immediately stormed back inside and sat down at his writing desk. He pulled out a telegram form, wrote for a few moments, then handed the cable to Luke. "Send that immediately! We'll put an abrupt halt to this nonsense."

Luke had been pleased at Ricker's response. At least the construction was still uppermost in the Colonel's mind. He read the telegram on the way out of the yard.

> HOOPER: WE DON'T WANT ANY MORE EXCURSIONS TO GLENWOOD UNTIL AFTER ROAD FINISHED. THE 13 CARS WE HAVE HERE HAS BOTHERED AND DELAYED US BEYOND ALL ACCOUNT WITH LIMITED ROOM. COL. R.E. RICKER

Ricker was correct. That should take care of the matter. He sent the cable from the new D&RG station. It was after dark, so he decided to board Star for the night and stay at the hotel. He checked his pockets first. At $3 a night, and an extra two bits for a bath, he would barely have enough money left for the remainder of the week.

On his way to the hotel, he saw Maribelle quietly walking along the main street, her arm tucked into the crook of another man's arm. "*Hardly a man,*" sniffed Luke. "*No more than a boy.*" Still, he nodded his head and tipped his hat when she looked his way.

She must not have seen him because she suddenly turned to her companion and began to speak in an animated fashion and laugh brightly. Her date seemed confused, but pleased. He smiled and tucked her arm closer to him. But it was the laughter that bothered Luke the most.

Dinner was a waste of money. The food was undercooked, and when he sent it back it returned nearly burned. It tasted strongly metallic. The entire event made him snappish. He retired early, but couldn't sleep. He lay awake in the darkness, listening to the people walk outside. Every soft voice stabbed at Luke, every laugh was a dagger. It took a long time to come to a decision, but there was no helping it. He knew what he had to do.

# CHAPTER 24

Luke stopped by Ricker's Special early in the morning. No response had come from Denver, but Ricker said he would advise the others when he heard back. Until he received a response, he warned, Luke and John should not be surprised to see more excursions.

"I don't trust Denver to not continue this trend," he said with annoyance. "They'll be hoping to capitalize on the novelty."

"If we built a siding at Satank, they would at least be out of our way," Luke said.

Ricker thought briefly and then nodded. "Very well, instruct Mr. Marshall to construct a siding. I will inform Denver that we will use Satank as a depot until the spur to Carbondale is complete. Also, I've sent Mr. Lamplaugh to the front. He's familiar with the status of supplies into Leadville. I believe he can assist."

It was a good thought, and Luke approved. Quimby held a great deal of power as the assistant superintendent of the entire western division. He could influence other stations where Luke and John couldn't.

A few minutes after leaving Ricker, Luke waited in the shadows near the edge of town. He watched as Maribelle approached the gate and opened it. He waited a few minutes longer, nervously shifting from foot to foot, then walked across to the house. He hesitated on the porch, closed hand raised to knock. He lowered his hand to his side. Was this truly what he wanted? Then he shook his head, annoyed. No! He could think of no other way to resolve the situation. He raised his hand once more.

The knock seemed much louder than it should. He took off his hat and smoothed his hair. Delicate, feminine footsteps sounded inside. When the door opened, he entered.

It was nearly a full hour later when Al Clark saw Luke riding slowly down the main street. The panic from earlier had been replaced by a cold, hollow feeling in Luke's stomach. He knew it would fade with time.

"Colonel Ballister?" Clark called. Luke turned to his voice. "Do you have a moment?"

Luke checked his pocket watch. If he didn't leave soon, he wouldn't make it back to the front today. "*Only* a moment, Al," he replied.

When Luke dismounted, Al handed him a tall stack of papers. "What's all this?" he asked.

Al looked at him tiredly. "Messages for the front. I had hoped you could take them with you to deliver. I've included copies of the messages John asked me to send. Ricker has informed me that the contractors are not to send messages to Emma by Western Union. The road hasn't completed setting the batteries to Satank, so this is the only way I can think to get them through."

Luke nodded and flipped through the telegrams. There must have been at least thirty messages! He nodded as he read a sampling. Twenty kegs of track washers, five of bolts, cross arms. "What of my four bridles?" Luke asked.

Al made an exasperated sound. "Nobody mentioned you needed bridles. I'm sending a message to Henry Acord in Gypsum now and can add that to the list." He removed a scrap of paper from his vest and added the note. "Alright, so I have one No. 9 frog, one switch stand, two single throw head chairs, one connecting rod, and three bridles."

"Four," corrected Luke. Al scratched out the number and re-wrote it. "I just found out that Allender needs more hay. I didn't get the message until after Engine 403 left for the front. Let him know that I'll get it on the next train. He asked for grain as well, but I have none to send. I'll have to wire for more."

Luke nodded. "Need anything else before I head back?"

Al looked at him nervously. "Actually, yes," he said. "I know it's not your problem, but our man George is quite ill. He's Bill McLeod's cousin. I told George he needs to see the town doctor, but he hasn't got the money. I'm tapped out as well, and the doctor doesn't extend credit. But, I'm afraid it might be influenza. He's in bad shape."

Luke sighed. "Let's see your man. I've only a few dollars left myself. But if he really needs help, I might be able to manage it."

George had a room at the boarding house. The plainly furnished front room was stifling hot, yet George sat in front of the fireplace, bundled under several blankets. His thin face was pale, except for the bright fever spots that blazed on his cheeks.

He looked up at them with rheumy eyes, then exploded into a fit of coughing that came from deep in his chest. Both Luke and Al instinctively stepped back.

"How you feelin' today, George?" Al asked softly.

"Poorly," George said, huddling deeper into the blankets. "Quite poorly, Al."

"George," Al said, "This is Colonel Ballister with the D&RG. He's going to give your message to Bill." George nodded to Luke, but did not extend his hand.

"My thanks to you, Colonel," he said with a rasping wheeze. "I'll be well soon enough, but I know how Bill frets."

They left quickly to avoid catching the illness. "You're correct, Al," Luke said after a moment. "Your man needs to see a doctor right away." He reached down and tucked fingers into a small pocket sewn inside his boot. He always kept one coin for emergencies. This seemed to qualify. He handed the gold ten dollar piece to Al. "Bring the town physician to him and buy whatever medicine he needs. I'll have McLeod repay the loan. I think you should have someone keep watch over him, though."

Al nodded. "Perhaps Bill can send his brother, Frank, down, or someone else. Could you ask him? His whole family has the sweet fever, so there's plenty of people on the road to assist. They all follow the rails like dogs after their master." He uttered a short laugh. "Even his dear mother works in a ticket office!"

"Best write it down," Luke replied, "With the many other matters, I wouldn't want to forget." Al stepped into the road's telegraph station to get a piece of paper for the note. Since the station had just opened, Luke decided to stop by the Western Union office at the other end of town to check for messages. Plus, he needed to send a personal telegram.

It was a wise decision. After accepting Luke's quickly written message, and his last dollar, the telegraph clerk in the tiny cage handed another stack of messages to the pair. "I've heard a number of messages going through to Aspen for McMurtrie, Al. Thought you should know."

"Aspen?" Clark exclaimed. "McMurtrie's at Emma, not Aspen!"

"Messages are going to 'end of track,' and that's Aspen," the clerk replied from behind the steel bars. "I can't intercept them, but you might want to check that station. There's been several just this morning." The telegraph chattered briefly, and the clerk stopped to listen. He turned and made several quick taps in response. The machine began to click again. "Sorry, Sirs, I've got to get back to work. I'll send your message as soon as I finish this one, Colonel." They left him tapping madly and scratching down letters on a pad with his other hand.

"Blazes!" Al exclaimed as they left the station. "How am I supposed to work when people can't find me? I've sent messages to every station between here and Pueblo. If they're replying to Aspen, I'll never get answers to my queries!"

"Let me see what I can do," Luke said, and headed for the train yard. He shook his head as he rode past the location where the new depot would stand. The materials still had not been located. Another trace had been put on.

He stopped by Ricker's Special once more, but the Colonel was not there. Instead, he talked to the conductor for Ricker's cars. "He'll not be back until much later. Can I give him a message?"

"Yes," Luke replied. "see if we can request that the uptown office repeat the Aspen business at Glenwood for the contractors. If the messages arrive in both places, they might actually receive them."

The conductor wrote down the message and left it for Ricker to find. Luke watched as Engine 83 was finishing hooking up cars for the front. He decided to hitch a ride. It would give him a chance to review the condition of the track and see where corrections needed to be made.

As they passed the Satank station, the boxcar Luke rode in suddenly began to sway and bounce. Luke barely managed to keep his footing and Star stumbled and slammed heavily against the wall. Her bridle jingled as she shook her head. The train slowed to a crawl as the rocking continued. "*What is the problem with this section?*" he wondered. When he arrived at the front, he posed the question to McMurtrie.

"It's that blamed short rail stock Gypsum is sending," John said with annoyance. "They're wobbling too much. We'll have to add more ballast, and keep the trains under twenty miles an hour for the time being. I'm hoping you brought the iron cars I've been waiting for. We might have time to replace that rail with longer stock."

Luke shook his head. "I'm afraid not," he replied. "All we brought is more of the short stock. But one of these cables says that the cars of steel have left Chicago, and are heading this way on the UP." He handed John the stack of telegrams. He stared at the pile of messages in awe.

"There's more at Aspen, I'm afraid," Luke said apologetically. "The 'End of Track' messages are being sent to Aspen instead of Glenwood. I've asked Ricker to instruct messages be sent both places, but someone will need to check with the Aspen station to see what's arrived."

"I swear I'm going to be in a killing mood by the end of this project, Luke!" McMurtrie exclaimed as he flipped through the messages. "No rail, no connectors, no fishplates! I don't have anywhere for my men to sleep or eat! My stock is starving, I don't have estimates from the engineers, and the bridge at Frying Pan is constructed all wrong! How am I supposed to build a railroad under these conditions?"

Luke had no answers. He was just as frustrated. He glanced away to see Quimby Lamplaugh striding up to the pair. "Haven't spoken to you for a number of years, Colonel Ballister!" Lamplaugh said heartily as he extended his hand. "I saw you at the Glenwood celebration, but you disappeared before we could talk."

Luke shook his hand. "Good to see you, Quimby. I'm pleased you could get away from your duties to help us complete this line."

"This line *is* my duty, Colonel! I'll be out of a job if the revenues don't increase," he said. He turned to McMurtie. "John, I'm going to request another engine. The work trains are short of power. Any word on the iron cars? We'll be out of rail in a few minutes."

"There's another day's worth at the Glenwood yard," Luke said. "And we've brought more of the short stock with us."

"And perhaps did you bring enough connectors this time?" asked a familiar voice behind Luke. He turned to see Edward O'Malley, looking annoyed.

"I thought you were working for Ballard's group," Luke said in greeting.

"I was, and will be again," Edward said. "But the tunnel is complete, and he hasn't word on the next project. Also," he said, a bit sheepishly. "I could not bear to have the first engine arrive without seeing it meself." Luke smiled as Edward continued. "Mr. McMurtrie has kindly offered me a post. I've my own crew!" he said proudly. Luke nodded his congratulations.

"What's this about the connectors, O'Malley?" John asked.

"They've sent enough short stock for the distance, but only as many connectors as are needed for the long," Edward said, returning to his previous annoyance. "I'll need half again as many connectors, or the work will stop. We've made mile post twelve today, but will go no further without supplies."

Quiet rain began to patter on the group. Luke looked up. The grey clouds that appeared every day about this time seemed unusually heavy. He blinked his eyes suddenly as the patter became a downpour, and he tipped his hat down over his forehead.

The workers ignored the rain. Luke found McLeod and delivered the message about George. Bill was grateful to Luke for the loan, and repaid it immediately. Soon, Frank McLeod was on his way to Glenwood to help his cousin.

By nightfall, it was impossible to set ties in the slimy brown mud. The entire crew of nearly a hundred crowded into the few bunk and dining cars. Edward proudly sought shelter in the bunk car containing the other crew bosses. Thunder boomed and rain drenched the work-site for hours. The crew slept wherever they could. Floors, tables, and benches became beds. When morning came, the rain had not lessened.

"Aye! And just look at what the water is doing to me lovely roadbed," Edward said, shaking his head sadly. Luke used his hand to wipe away the steam on the window from the tightly packed bodies inside the car. He looked to see where Edward was staring. He was right. The downpour was digging deep furrows, and washing away the ballast! Luke's stomach clenched with a dreadful suspicion.

He pushed his way to the end of the car and stepped out into the storm. "Where are you going?" John shouted from the platform. Luke didn't respond. He bent his head into the blinding torrent and held his hat down tight. Lightning flashed overhead. Thunder boomed. He fought the wind, walking backward along the track. He was breathing hard and his battered ribs ached from the effort. He stopped when he reached the area where the train had bucked and swayed yesterday. A waterfall was crashing over the top of the new cut in the hillside, sweeping earth and rocks before it. With nothing to stop or divert the flow, the water was etching a channel across the raised bed.

A small tree uprooted and crashed down across the tracks, landing in the field below. The racing water and debris had already unseated a number of ties. A section of the short rail dipped and twisted precariously. Quickly as he could, Luke made his way back to the bunk car. He shook the water from his hat before he entered.

"We've got to get a crew out to section ten," he announced. "There's a waterfall coming over the edge of the cliff. The water's washed away the bed. The 403 will be arriving from Glenwood soon. It won't see the damage in this storm until it's too late!"

"They got the batteries set yesterday at Satank," John said. "We'll ride down and wire Glenwood to hold the work train."

Luke shook his head. "Check your watch, John. They already left a half hour ago. We don't have much time!"

John hesitated. "Maybe they'll spot the damage," he said. "If it's obvious enough . . . ."

"It would never occur to them to look, and you know it! The only reason I thought of it was because of how much the train shook on the section yesterday. I didn't think the light ballast would stand up to the rain, much less a waterfall!"

Edward had been listening quietly. "The good Colonel's correct," he said in a booming voice that stopped all other conversation in the car. "If the work train hits a twisted section, it'll derail to be sure. We've not time to right it if we hope to beat the Midland."

Panic moved from man to man. They all knew Luke was correct, but it would take every man they had to dam the flow and fix the track. "I'll head down a mile or so and flag the train if I can," Luke said. "But if it doesn't see me . . . ." He left the sentence uncompleted.

John pulled his heavy coat from a cupboard. "We'll get the rails fixed. Come on, men!"

Luke grabbed a red lantern, lit it, and headed for the cliff overhang that protected the corral. He grabbed a bridle and saddle and tossed them on Star. The other animals milled nervously as the thunder and lightning cracked, but Star waited patiently as Luke slowly mounted. His arm was growing numb again, so he held the reins with his left hand. He lashed the lantern to his saddle in case he lost all use of his right arm. As men poured from the rail cars bearing picks and shovels, Luke spurred Star sharply. "Hey-up!" he shouted over the noise of the pounding rain.

Star bounded into the storm, her shod hooves raising furious splashes. Turning onto the rough road that paralleled the rails, she skidded on the slick surface. Although she regained her footing quickly, the sudden movement made Luke catch his breath as his ribs twisted agonizingly. His head began to pound from the pain, and it became difficult to see where he was going. The half frozen rain stung his hands and face. Star seemed to know what he wanted and kept going in a straight path, following the rails.

Luke could hear the faint whistle of the train as it passed the Satank station. The 403 must have left the station early. It would be here in a few minutes, and he wasn't nearly a mile from the damaged rails. He grabbed the lantern, dismounted, and left Star to find shelter near the cliff face. He turned up the flame until the red glass blazed, and began to swing it in wide arcs from side to side. The movement was nearly too much for his injured ribs to handle. He took short, gasping breaths and continued swinging the lantern. Minutes passed. The roadbed began to shake as the engine approached.

The ice-cold torrent poured down mercilessly. Luke couldn't see through the storm, but knew the train was almost upon him. The headlight appeared out of nowhere, far too close. Startled, Luke leapt to the side, leaving the lantern on the tracks, and rolled down the embankment. He stopped just short of a stream formed by the rain, nearly the size and speed of the Roaring Fork. He could barely move by the time he halted his fall. He lay there, pain flooding his mind, wheezing heavily. He struggled against the darkness that ate at the edge of his vision, listening intently. A heartbeat later, a whistle pierced the air. They had seen him! But, if they had not understood the warning, it would still be too late. When the first scream of the brakes reached his ears, he would have breathed a sigh of relief — if only he could breathe.

# Chapter 25

"Nothing done today. Raining since last night at 430 P.M. — too muddy to work this P.M.," John wrote. He folded the cable, and tucked it in his pocket to take it to Satank to wire. He looked over at Luke who lay on his bunk. Even with a fresh bandage tightly wrapped around his torso, the man could barely take a breath without coughing.

"It's probably for the best," John said consolingly. "You need to rest those ribs. Skel says you've broken two of them for sure this time, and cracked another." John shook his head in wonder. "Damned amazing that you stopped that train, Luke. She was loaded up and had a full head of steam on her. They almost didn't see you. If you hadn't of stood right on the tracks, they would have passed you by."

"Fine day they picked to run early," Luke commented. His voice was a hoarse rasp. He'd caught cold in addition to the new injury to his ribs.

"At least we've now received the supplies we need," John said. "They've unloaded 30,000 ties outside the big tunnel, and we've got enough fifty-two pound stored at Glenwood and Satank to get nearly to the Aspen yard." He looked out into the continuing rain. "If this blasted rain would just stop, we could get back to laying track."

"We should turn over some of the crew to Parker's telegraph gang. Poles should be easy to set in this muck," Luke said. He raised a fist to his mouth and coughed, after which he moaned lightly.

"Set — yes," replied John. "Stabilize — no. But you're right. We should get the holes dug, at least. The men are getting restless. Blast it, we need those extra bunk cars! The tents are useless in this downpour. I've got forty-one men crowded into three bunk cars and the fistfights are escalating."

"No word on the cars yet?" Luke asked, slowly turning his head to look at his friend. He had done his neck no favor in the most recent fall.

"Quimby says they've been sent forward from Salida, but they're lost somewhere out there," John said in frustration. "Probably loaded with Allender's grain," he added with a brittle laugh. "By the way Luke, I'm heading to Aspen after I send this report. We're starting to build the yard, and I want to make sure the bridge is ready to receive rail. Soon as the line is in, we'll need to bring over a round table and water tank so we can manage the engines. And if time's not already tight, I was just informed they're going to run the Aspen business to Emma instead of Satank!"

"But we just finished putting in the siding in Satank!" Luke replied with a note of frustration.

John shook his head and threw up his hands. "I know! But there's a better *hotel* at Emma, and the stage line already runs there. I can't even reach Marshall today to tell him. He's at Carbondale."

Luke nodded. "I'll let him know. We've got the materials already, so we can probably have it done on Sunday. They can start to run business there by Monday night, if we hurry."

"I appreciate it," John replied before stepping out into the storm. Luke considered rising and checking on progress but he knew Skel might have him forcibly returned to his bunk if he did so. Yet another day he wouldn't receive pay! Eventually, he closed his eyes and slept through to the next morning.

The following day, the skies finally cleared. Luke could see his breath as he started to work. The ground had a thin layer of frost. The men struggled to work in the cold, slimy muck. More than one worker ended up on his tail after slipping. The weight of the rich silt that stuck to boots and pant legs further burdened the crew.

The cold air didn't help Luke's chest cough. He didn't feel feverish, but he was worried about his exposure to George's illness. Bill had informed him that George was even worse. The medicine wasn't helping. Bill had sent another ten dollars for the doctor, but Frank reported no progress.

Luke wrapped his hands around his coffee mug, letting the heat seep into his fingers. The tracks were nearing Frying Pan, and the route was graded to the cañon at Snowmass Creek. Word had reached the crew that the Midland was nearly to Frying Pan. It seemed to energize the men when they arrived at Bridge Number Two, and saw the Midland graders coming down the Frying Pan valley. With shouts and oaths, his men began to work like beavers. Many did not stop for lunch. Luke planned to take full advantage of their competitive nature.

The following day, the temperature dropped faster. Twice in the night, one of his fellows had gotten up to stoke the stove in the bunk car. Again, the men were forced to sleep two to a bunk, and on the benches in the dining car, just to stay warm.

By midday, the cañon at Snowmass Creek was in sight. Luke stood on the platform of the bunk car and, just for a moment, allowed himself to appreciate the beauty of the valley. The aspen trees that had blazed yellow for over a week were nearly bereft of leaves now. The scrub oaks dotting the hillsides were still a brilliant red. The tops of the mountains received a blanket of snow from the rains that buffeted the valley each day. The snow glistened in the sunlight. The air was growing thinner as they rose in elevation. Now the hardest push was upon them. He hoped they reached Aspen before the snow flew in earnest.

Charlie Sullivan walked by the platform as Luke finished his midday meal, chuckling to himself. "At least someone is cheerful," Luke said, his voice still rasping.

Sullivan turned and looked up at Luke with twinkling eyes. "I suppose I should be angry, but it's just so blamed ridiculous!"

"What is?" Luke asked curiously.

Charlie held up a slip of paper. "I wired Mr. Lamplaugh to ask him for working tent stoves as the ones we have now are useless. He replied that he has none, and then asks me to send him one of *our* bunk cars!"

Luke made a startled sound, somewhere close to laugh. "I hope you said no!"

"'Course I did!" Sullivan exclaimed. "Quimby should know better! I need *more* space, not less! We still haven't seen the extra bunk cars we requested weeks ago. I'm sending a reply right now."

Luke left Charlie to his mission and returned to his desk inside. Bill McLeod stopped by a bit later while Luke was writing reports. "Mr. McMurtrie asked me to check with you to see if you need assistance with any tasks. I'm grateful for your help with George, so if there's anything I can do, just ask."

Luke's turned to him and asked, "How *is* George? Any improvement?"

"Oh, yes, Sir! Frank says he's up and moving around. The medicine the doctor gave him finally worked. I hope to see him at the celebration in Aspen!"

Luke smiled. "Could you check to see what wires have arrived today? I know that Parker has set the batteries to Emma, but I'm not certain they're run to Frying Pan."

"I'd be happy to, Sir."

After McLeod left, Luke re-read yesterday's personal telegram from Denver. The freight he had ordered would be placed on the work train, and should be delivered by November first. He breathed a sigh of relief. At last he could resolve the issue with Maribelle.

McLeod returned a few hours later with a stack of telegrams. Luke scanned them briefly. "Bill, let Allender know that Clark is sending fifty sacks of oats and twenty-five bales of hay for him." He flipped through the rest of the stack before Bill left. "Also, please give this message to Mr. King." McLeod hurried to his tasks, leaving Luke to complete his reports.

A few minutes later, he was startled to hear King's voice outside the car. "They're mad, I tell you! Completely daft!" As Frank King raised his bulky frame into the bunk car, the car rocked visibly. "Colonel, can't you do something?" He waved the cable in front of Luke's nose.

"I didn't read the cable, Frank. What are they asking now?"

King waved his hands madly, barely missing Luke's head and the edge of the cabinet overhead. "They say that Bridge Number Two over the Roaring Fork is too long!"

"Is it?" Luke asked reasonably.

"Of course it is!" King snarled. "The bank wouldn't stabilize. I tried to fill it with material, Colonel. Truly I did! The men were hauling fill over 1500 feet. I determined that it was costing us sixty cents a yard to haul the fill! Lengthening the bridge was much more economical!" King's face grew redder with each statement, and his hands waved more wildly.

After ducking another arm movement at a cost to his ribs, Luke said, "Then simply tell Ricker that, Frank. If you give him the numbers, he'll realize the cost savings."

"He doesn't trust my judgment," King grumbled.

"Of course not, Frank!" Luke replied with a hearty laugh. "Colonel Ricker doesn't trust any judgment other than his own!" He smiled at the heavy man, and was rewarded with a small chuckle.

"As you say, Colonel! Very well," King said. "I'll wire him the details immediately. Thank you so much, Colonel!" He forcibly grabbed Luke's hand and shook it fervently before he left the boxcar like a whirlwind. Luke could only shake his head in wonder. How did that man ever become an engineer?

He swung down from the bunk car and strode over to the bridge. The workers were just laying tracks across it. Luke certainly couldn't fault Ricker for wondering about the bridge. It appeared to be twice as long as necessary. Still, he did trust Frank's judgment. It certainly wouldn't do to have a loaded engine go into the river. He had just turned and started back to the office when he heard Edward exclaim, "Begorry! Jacob, Pat, get off of there!! The rest of you, get back!"

Luke spun around as a sharp, cracking sound came from the bridge. He watched as the trestle began to sway. Huge chunks of dirt began to slough from the opposite bank of the river, and then from the closer bank. Soon the bridge was freestanding, except for the twin rains and ties already spiked to them. The two men Edward had called back stood uncertainly near the middle of the trestle, still carrying the sledges they'd used to hammer spikes. Luke raced forward to the bank.

He felt movement underfoot and stepped back quickly. Edward did the same. Another piece of bank sloughed into the river below with a loud crash. Although it wasn't a very long drop to the water, the river was running fast, and was cold enough that Luke doubted the men would be able to survive to reach the shore.

The two men started to walk toward them. The trestle piers swayed. They should have been much sturdier! The tie closest to Luke began to rock and raise from the bed. The men froze in place. "What'll we do, Colonel?" one man shouted.

"Don't do anything! Just stand there for a moment while we figure this out!" Luke called back.

"King!" Luke yelled over his shoulder. "Get over here!" He heard pounding footsteps as Frank King reached the pair.

King shook his head in annoyance. "I knew it! I should have made it longer still! You see what I mean now, Colonel? Stabilizing this soil is almost impossible. I'll start the calculations immediately to determine the new lengths necessary!" He started to turn to run back to the camp.

Luke stared incredulously. "*Frank*!!" he called.

The man stopped and turned. "Yes, Colonel?"

Luke gestured to the bridge. "The *men*? How do I get them off of there?"

Frank walked forward and noticed, for the first time, the men standing on the bridge. He shrugged. "I've no idea, Colonel," he said, pursing his lips. Luke put a hand to his forehead, while Edward swore under his breath.

Shouts and calls came from across the river. The men of the Midland were cheering the damage to the bridge. They taunted and yelled. The D&RG men responded with oaths and threats. Jacob and Pat took a few warning steps in the direction of the Midland crew until the bridge started to sway once more. The Midland men laughed and hooted. In a few minutes, however, the novelty was over and the Midland's grading crew returned to their work, more ferverantly than before.

Luke looked over the situation carefully. He walked downstream a bit and peered over the edge. "Why are those piers so unsteady?" he called to King.

"As I said, Colonel," the ruddy-faced man said as he came closer to where Luke stood, "the soil is unstable. We've set the piers down to bedrock, but that's quite near the surface in this area."

"Is there anything we can do to *make* them more stable? If we can, the men can simply walk out on the ties."

"If they walk off then the entire bridge could collapse into the river, and we'll have to begin again," Frank countered.

"Which is *why* I asked if we can make the piers more sturdy!" Luke said, struggling to control his temper.

"Chapman is in Aspen. I can wire him or I can try to wire Denver and see if the bridge department has any ideas. I'm sure we can have a solution in a few days," King offered.

Luke gave an exasperated sigh. "Let me try to make you understand this, Frank. It's nearing dark. The temperatures will drop below freezing tonight. Those men need to come off the bridge immediately, and we must fix the piers today before the work train can cross it to continue the tracks *tomorrow*." Luke stared at him, willing him to understand the urgency of the situation. He directed King's attention to the opposite side of the river. "Those men across the way are the Midland graders. Now," he continued, "what is our best hope of accomplishing both of the tasks before us *right now*?"

King appeared startled when Luke pointed out the Midland crew. His face took on a thoughtful look and he began to nod. "Yes, of course, Colonel! I understand your concern. We must resolve this situation with all due haste!" He began to walk away from the bridge, staring up at the cliffs. "Yes, yes," he muttered, "That could work nicely. Yes, and that one, too."

"Mr. King?" Luke asked. When the engineer didn't respond, he said it again, louder, "*Frank!*"

King turned, startled. "Yes, Colonel?"

"The plan, Frank?" Luke asked, arms spread.

"Oh, yes! Of course," he said, and moved back toward Luke. He leaned close enough that his head was almost at Luke's ear. "Now, I should first tell you that the manner in which those piers are wobbling is not natural." He started to continue, when Luke stopped him with a gesture.

"What did you say?" Luke wanted to be very certain he understood the implication raised.

King lowered his voice even further. "I'm saying that the difficulty with the piers must have had assistance," he said. "I designed this bridge, and I watched Mr. Chapman put in the footers for those piers. Of course, it's impossible to see what has been damaged under the water, but I assure you it could easily have withstood a fully loaded coal train before today!"

Luke took in this information, as he looked thoughtfully at the crew of the Midland on the other side of the river.

"However, Colonel, I believe that I have a solution!"

Luke turned back to see King's face beaming. He motioned for the man to continue.

"If the men removed that boulder," he said, pointing to a large chunk of granite on the mountainside, "as well as that one, and the one right next to it," he continued, pointing to two more stones, "we could place them in the water to shore up the piers."

"Will it support the *train*, without fail?" Luke asked suspiciously.

"It will allow the *men* to come off the trestle," King said pointedly, "I will begin work immediately to design the extra supports necessary to replace the bank so the *train* may pass tomorrow. We'll likely have to work all night, but by morning it should be complete!"

Luke nodded. Working through the night might be best if, in fact, saboteurs were at work. "Will your design also take into account *future* efforts to dismantle the bridge?" Luke asked significantly.

King's eyes narrowed. His face took on a cold, hard look that Luke had not seen on the man before. "I was not aware I was designing the bridge to withstand sabotage. However, I can assure you, Colonel, that I am fully capable of ensuring that this bridge will continue to stand for years to come! Many of my bridges are the only things that remain in areas that were devastated by war."

Luke nodded curtly. "Very well," he said. "Please tell the men what they need to do, and begin the designs immediately. Because, make no mistake, we *will* continue this line tomorrow."

# CHAPTER 26

"Maribelle! Mind your cooking!" Abigail Johnson stood in the door of the tiny kitchen with hands on her hips.

Maribelle looked up from where she sat at the table, head in hands. The pot of soup was boiling over. It hissed and steamed as it hit the hot stove top. "Oh!" she exclaimed, standing and rushing forward.

Abigail lifted the pot from the stove, using her long apron to pad the handles while Maribelle reached for another cloth to wipe the thick soup from the stove surface. Abigail glared at her daughter but Maribelle couldn't meet her mother's eyes. Tears brimmed close to the surface. Mrs. Johnson sighed and shook her head. It was frustrating, and heartbreaking to watch.

"I'm sorry, Mama," Maribelle said softly as she pumped water into the sink to rinse the cloth. "I wasn't paying proper attention." Cold water rushed over her hands, chilling them. She placed them over her eyes for a moment, and felt the coolness stem the tears.

Abigail walked behind Maribelle and placed gentle hands on her shoulders. "You've been downhearted for weeks now Maribelle. Is it still that railroad man who fills your heart?"

"I can't help it, Mama," Maribelle sighed. "I thought . . . and then, to have him introduce me to another man at the celebration — as though I was a steer at auction — it made me feel . . . ." She couldn't finish.

Abigail slid her arms around her daughter's waist and hugged her tight. "Perhaps he thought he was doing a kindness," she offered hesitantly.

Maribelle broke away and spun around. "A *kindness*!" she exclaimed, then placed her hands on her hips. "Well! There are certainly better ways to tell a woman she should not depend on a man's affections." She fiercely turned back to the sink and picked up the cloth once more. She stared at it for a moment, then rested her hands on the edge of the basin. Her head dropped and she closed her eyes. As hard as she tried to be angry, the hurt and sadness returned. "He's not even contacted me since the celebration, Mama," she whispered. "Not to apologize, nor even had the courtesy to formally end the courtship."

Once again Abigail hugged her daughter from behind. "It'll turn out for the best, Maribelle. You'll see." Maribelle turned and returned the hug.

# CHAPTER 27

Edward removed his heavy coat and sat down on one of the benches in the dining car with his plate of food. Jacob and Pat were talking animatedly.

"I plan to buy some land with my bonus," Pat said. "And perhaps a few fine sheep."

Jacob laughed. "This is cattle country, Patrick Coughlin! If it's sheep you're wanting, perhaps you should return to Ireland."

"I could, if I had a mind, Jacob O'Toole!" Pat replied strongly. "I could own me own pub, and I'd not let you drink!" The two men laughed uproariously.

"I'll be bringing my beautiful Maggie to be with me once more," Edward said softly. "Ah! How I miss her shining, black hair. And her laugh!"

"Then Mr. McMurtrie will be paying a bonus, as well?" Pat asked. "I'd not heard that from your fellows."

Edward stopped abruptly, the fork nearly to his mouth. He turned wide, panicked eyes to his friend. A chill settled over his heart and he was suddenly cold in the warmth of the dining car.

He'd started on this project when the road had announced an end bonus. With the wages and the reward he could bring Maggie to this new country. They would buy a piece of land and be their own masters. Tommy had hoped to do the same for his mum. But when Tommy died, and Mr. Ballard had offered the higher post . . . he'd been too overcome with emotions to think straight. Later, when he'd gotten his own crew, he'd been filled with pride. Oh, pride! It truly was the seed of evil!

"I've ruined us," he whispered. He had thought only of himself, not of his family. Once again, he'd failed them! "How could I forget about the bonus?"

Pat and Jacob looked at their stricken friend. "Perhaps if you asked Mr. McMurtrie?" Pat offered. "He's a good man. You might be able to make an arrangement."

"Had I approached him when I accepted the post, then perhaps," Edward said, shaking his head. He finally laid down the fork with the uneaten food. "But no, I've no one but meself to blame. It was hard enough to tell me dear sister of Tommy. Now, I'll have to either tell Maggie of this new failure, or return home in shame." He looked down at his food, still barely touched. "I think I'll be returning to work now," he said, and pushed away the plate.

"Your shift has ended, Edward," Pat said. "You need to rest."

Edward stood and looked down at his friends. Self-anger filled his face. "I'll not rest again until we finish. If I'm working, I canna think. The sooner we reach Aspen, the sooner I can go home."

Jacob looked at him with bemusement. "You can't work the entire time, Edward. You'd drop in your tracks. We've another six days to reach Aspen. Perhaps more!"

"I've done it before," Edward said stubbornly, putting on his coat. He turned, and over his shoulder said, "And I'll do it again."

Pat exhaled a short burst of air in disbelief and raised his brows. "I'd pay good money to see that!" he exclaimed.

Jacob joined in with spirit. "As would I. I've a mind to place a wager on the matter."

Edward stopped in his tracks at the words. He turned and looked at his smirking friends. "And would ye, now?" he asked slyly. A thought had begun to form in the back of his mind. His friends caught the look. They turned to each other and grinned. "I'll call the boys!" exclaimed Jacob quickly.

"So it's decided, then?" Jacob asked the group of men. "Each of you will wager ten dollars against what money Edward has saved that he can remain working for the next six days, without rest?"

"I say until we reach Aspen, whenever that may be!" exclaimed Frank O'Rourke, who had just returned from seeing the company doctor in Denver for his hand.

Pat looked at Edward, who nodded. "Aye! Whether six days, or ten, I'll remain standing."

Heads shook in disbelief. "You'll never manage it, Edward!" another exclaimed.

Edward pushed through the crowd and stood right next to the speaker, towering over him. "And would you be doubting me solemn oath then, John Reilly?" The smaller man shrugged, but said no more.

"I've no doubt you can remain working for the time, Edward!" exclaimed O'Rourke. "You're a crew boss now and merely sit on your duff all day!" The group all laughed, including Edward. "Now, if you were back *beside* us, actually *working* each day . . . ." he offered slyly, "I might be willing to double my bet."

When the rest of the assembled men agreed with shouts and cheers, Edward looked uneasy. "I've responsibilities, lads," he said hesitantly. "The good Mr. McMurtrie has hired me for a post. I don't know if he would be willing to allow me your terms . . . ."

"You want to do *what*?" John McMurtrie exclaimed minutes later as Edward watched him uncomfortably.

"I'd forgotten about the bonus the road is paying," Edward began. John put up his hand to stop him.

"I don't have the money to pay bonuses, Edward. I'm sorry."

"And well do I understand, Sir," Edward replied quickly. "But the goal is reaching Aspen, is it not?" When McMurtrie nodded, he continued. "The lads have wagered whether I can remain working the rails until we reach Aspen, without sleep and without food. I believe I can, and their wagers could replace the bonus."

John looked at the bigger man. The men were all tired, and getting irritable. This wager business might distract them and keep up morale. He'd seen Edward work long hours without even blinking. He narrowed his eyes.

"Who would give me my reports if you're on the crew?" he asked. Although Edward could not read, nor write, he'd given excellent oral reports up to this point.

Edward had anticipated the objection and had a ready answer. "The Chinese headman you've hired from Mr. Ballard, Li Sung, could give the reports in my stead." He owed the man a favor for helping him compose the letter to Katie about Tommy. Li had suggested they describe Tommy's death as an accident — a hazard of the job. It had taken a great load from Edward's mind. Too, there was that business in the tunnel . . . .

McMurtrie raised his brows. "I need the reports in *English*, Edward."

"Aye! And well can he speak and scribe the language. He writes as well as any English solicitor!"

John pursed his lips. "I'll speak to the man. If he can do what you say, I'll allow the bet. However, I insist you be allowed meals. I'll not have my men starving in the field. With that amendment, you may proceed."

A chorus of boos had greeted the amendment. "It was his firm requirement," Edward said. "Otherwise, the wager cannot ole."

Pat Coughlin, looking down at the handful of money so far collected, said, "What if he remains standing while he eats? Then he's not resting a bit." The men mulled over the possibility.

Frank O'Rourke nodded. "Very well then, but we'll want someone to verify that he's working each full shift, as some of us will be sleeping," he said, scratching at his bandage despite the doctor's orders. The others nodded.

# CHAPTER 28

The rails had reached Woody Creek. Luke was supervising the loading of the pile driver on a flatbed, so that it could be taken to the Satank spur in Section twenty-four. He heard an oath behind him, and looked over to see Edward swinging his sledge in a wide arc. He hit the spike slightly off-kilter and the head of the hammer slipped, nearly causing the man to fall. His partner stepped back quickly. Luke looked carefully at Edward. The man was exhausted! Luke had been spending his time working on completing the spur into the Carbondale station, and hadn't been to the front in several days. He looked over to where John McMurtrie stood, reading the telegrams Luke had brought.

"John!" he called, and McMurtrie stopped and joined Luke where he stood. "When is the last time that man rested?" he asked, pointing at Edward. They watched the man again try to hammer the spike. It drove in over an inch from the blow. Edward shook his head as if to clear the cobwebs.

John shook his head in amazement. "Over four days, and counting! The side wagers are growing." He leaned closer to Luke and said in a consipiratory manner. "Odds are two to one. I've put five on him myself! I think he'll make it the whole way!"

At Luke's questioning look, John explained the bet, as well as the reason. Luke watched the man again. "Four days, now?"

John nodded, and then said, "It's a good thing he can do the work of three men, because none of the others are worth their salt right now!"

Luke pursed his lips. They only had another twelve miles to reach the tracks coming out of Aspen. He reached into his pocket and flipped a gold coin to John. "Give this to whoever is holding the money. Edward to win."

John smiled and tucked it into his pocket.

Luke turned, then winced as the big Irishman missed a swing, hitting the rail with a clang. "Although, John, I'd consider putting him on pushing carts. I'd hate for someone to get in the way of that hammer!"

Another day passed. Edward stood unsteadily as he ate his food, but he stood. He didn't taste the excellently seasoned stew; it was merely fuel. Pat Coughlin stood by protectively, herding him like a border collie. "Today you're pushing carts, Edward. You can do that, aye?" he asked.

"Aye," Edward said tiredly. "How many more miles, Pat?" He slurred.

"Just seven, Edward. Most all of the men have bought in now. Even the other contractors! You'll have your bonus, with some to spare."

"Aye," Edward said again automatically. The words didn't quite register, but he was happy that Pat was excited by whatever he just said. He had gotten his instructions, however. He was pushing carts. He lumbered toward the end of the track, Pat at his heels like a nervous hen.

Edward was well past exhausted. He could barely think. But his arms and legs were still strong, still responding to the simple commands he gave. Push, dump, then return and repeat. The actions consumed his every thought. The hours slipped by, as the track lengthened.

"So, that's the situation, men," Luke said the following day. "I'll leave it to you. How do I reply to Leadville?"

Pat Coughlin spoke up from the crowd gathered around Luke near the dining car. He kept watch on Edward out of the corner of his eye. "You're saying we can reach Aspen by November first, just two days from now if the last supply train comes forward, or another day will pass if the pay train is flagged through?"

When Luke nodded, Pat said strongly to the others. "I say the pride is worth waiting a day for pay! Let the work train flag past!" Several men called out a cheer of agreement.

John Reilly responded the challenge. "You only say that because you've wagered for Edward to finish. I'm entitled to my pay, Patrick Coughlin! Your man will just have to stand another day. The pay train must come through!" A smaller group of men voiced their concurrence. The two groups slowly split and stood facing each other.

"You've no heart, John Reilly!" called one man.

"And you've no *brain*!" responded Frank O'Rourke fiercely, standing beside Reilly.

"Give the man a fighting chance, for the sake of Heaven!" exclaimed Pat Coughlin. "What harm will it do you?"

Luke watched the rising antagonism with alarm. He hadn't intended to start a war! Yet, if he interfered, it could cause even more strife, since the crew had learned Luke had bet on Edward to succeed. He shook his head, hoping calmer heads would prevail.

The men fell silent as Edward trudged through the center of the two groups. When he finally faced Luke, he said, "Let the pay train pass, if it must," he slurred through lips that would barely respond. His bloodshot eyes saw the Colonel blurrily. "I've made my oath, and

I'll stand by it. I'll not be the subject of such a conflict." Then he turned and slowly plodded back to his post, tripping over a small pile of rubble. He stopped, regained his balance and continued. The men all watched as he reached his cart once more. He pushed the massive cart, which normally took two men to move, with effort. Sweat poured from his brow, even in the chilly mountain air.

Pat Coughlin looked at Reilly and said with fire, "Take your gold then, John Reilly, and be damned with you! I still say Edward will prevail, despite your cold heart!" He turned and stormed away to help his friend with the cart.

The men standing behind Reilly looked to him. He glared after Edward with animosity, then he turned and looked at Luke. Finally, with a harsh breath of exasperation, he said, "Flag the work train, Colonel. I'll not be held to account if he were to fail because of it!" Reilly angrily pushed his way through the group of cheering men and returned to his work.

Edward's world narrowed to listening to Pat, pushing the rock cart, and keeping moving so his limbs would continue to function. It was getting difficult to breathe in the thin air, but the cold kept him awake. His fingers were numb through the thick gloves, and his nose was red and swollen. He hadn't dared to drink any whiskey to warm him. He couldn't afford to be sleepy.

He shook his head slightly as he pushed a cart past the caboose. Another of the engineers was ranting and raving. They were certainly an excitable lot!

"They've taken leave of their senses, Colonel!" exclaimed John Morton, who had replaced Frank King for the final assault on the mountain.

Luke struggled not to smile. King had said the same about Morton just a few short days before!

"How many miles do we have to finish, Colonel?" he asked, although he already knew the answer.

"Just four," Luke said carefully, not certain where John was leading.

"Look at this cable! Just look at it!" John shoved the paper at Luke. It was badly crinkled, as though it had already been crumpled into trash at least once. His brows raised as he read the few words.

"One-half percent!" Morton exclaimed. "They want me to achieve a one-half percent grade! Do the math yourself, Colonel! Forty two miles between Glenwood Springs and here, with a four thousand foot increase in elevation! Now, you tell me how I'm supposed to achieve half a percent in a rock cañon less than a mile across?" Morton stood, hands on hips, breathing hard and fast. "I'm to redesign an entire spur with just two days to connect the line?"

"Tell them it can't be done," Luke offered with a shrug.

"Excuse me?" Morton asked, his anger abruptly deflated.

Luke handed Morton the telegram back. "Simply inform Denver that the suggested grade can't be achieved." When Morton's look turned from glazed to sly, he cautioned, "But mind your tone, John. I can't afford to lose you at this point!"

He was relieved when Morton gave an exasperated sigh and nodded.

# CHAPTER 29

It was midday, and Edward was waiting for Pat, or one of the others, to return to watch him work after he had eaten his meal. He stood at his cart, staring at it, trying to comprehend why it was still empty. He looked around, realizing that he stood alone in the lightly falling snow. Where had everyone gone?

"We've done it, Edward!" Pat Coughlin exclaimed, rushing up to him. He clapped Edward on the shoulder, nearly knocking him over. "*You've done it!*" He turned his friend around, and caught him when he stumbled.

He swayed on his feet in the quickening breeze and strained to see where Pat was pointing. "It's Aspen, Edward! There's the yard!"

He saw the houses, but tired as he was, he couldn't be excited. He understood the impact, though. "Did we raise enough, Pat? Can my sweet Maggie-girl make passage?" The words were slow and barely recognizable.

Jacob joined the pair, beaming from ear to ear.

"Aye!" Pat exclaimed with a joyous laugh. "Your dear Maggie will have her own stateroom and eat dinner at the Captain's table! They'll call her Lady Margaret and bow before her!" He swept into an exaggerated courtly bow.

"Or you can bring along your sister, Kathleen, if you've a mind!" added Jacob.

Edward looked at them in wonder! Enough money to make passage for two? He found it hard to comprehend that much gold!

"As much as all that, then?" he asked softly. He struggled to understand, and his friend's looks softened.

"Get some sleep, Edward," Pat said warmly. "We've booked you a room at the finest hotel in Aspen! John Reilly is footing the bill, though he'll not like to be reminded of it!"

"And what of my winnings? Are they safe?" Edward asked. He'd not have the last week for naught.

"Aye!" Pat replied. "Mr. McMurtrie has your winnings guarded in his strongbox."

Jacob grinned at Edward. "We'll forgive you for missing the celebration, lad! But we'll toast your health and strength!"

# CHAPTER 30

"Freight for you, Colonel," George Moore called from the steps of the work train that had just pulled into the Aspen yard. He tossed down a small wooden box. Luke caught it quickly, his heart beating wildly. If it had broken . . . .

He opened the box and checked the contents. No damage. He breathed a sigh of relief and walked over to where John McMurtrie stood watching the work train move cars around the yard. John turned as Luke reached his side.

"The Special should be here soon, Luke. I'm sure President Moffat will be pleased with you! He'll probably toast you at the celebration. I wouldn't be surprised if Ricker even raised a glass. You've earned your bonus, and then some."

"And you earned your contract price, John. It was a task well done by all! But, I hope President Moffat doesn't intend to toast me, because I won't be here."

John looked at him with astonishment! "Won't *be* here!? After all this effort, you'll not attend the celebration?"

"I've a matter that requires my attention, John. I'll be hitching a ride with the work train to Satank, and then ride the remainder of the distance to Glenwood."

John nodded knowingly. "Well, then, I'll wish you well! We'll be working here at the yard for several more days, so I'm sure I'll see you before I return to Pueblo and see my family. I'll try to pry away one bottle from the crew for later."

Luke nodded. He took Star over to the livestock loading platform. He entered the boxcar with her for the trip down to Satank. Just then, the engineer blew his whistle three times, making Luke wince. Dugan apparently didn't know the whistle was the signal that the Special was about to arrive. He chuckled to himself as the Aspen townsfolk quickly began to light the paper Chinese lanterns that lined the streets. The food and drink began to flow.[5] He had no doubt that the food and much of the liquor would be gone long before the Special ever arrived.

The work train neared the first bridge, where it would begin to back onto the Carbondale siding so the Special could pass. Luke heard

Glen Fay's voice outside the end of the boxcar. "You'll have only six minutes to unload, Colonel, before we have to get off the platform."

Luke nodded and readied Star's saddle. He led her to the boxcar door and watched the landscape slowly go by as the trained passed by Bridge Number One. A pair of workers were quickly making repairs to the track near the bridge.

*"Odd. I thought all of the men were at the Aspen celebration."*

After he offloaded Star and mounted, he decided to take a moment to check on the working men. He neared the crest of the hill, and could see the tall plume of smoke from the Special as it departed Glenwood Springs. His attention returned to the two men working on the track. They were intent on their job and didn't notice him approach. Two wrenches lay on the ground near the men, and each held a long crowbar. As he watched, they fit the crowbars under the rail and began to pry it loose from the ties. Luke glanced again at the plume of smoke. The train would go right into the river. How many people would die?

He pulled his Colt and nudged Star forward until he was right behind the pair. "Stop where you are!" he exclaimed. The men froze. One of them quickly dropped the crowbar and reached for his gun. Luke shot him in the calf.

The man dropped to the ground and rolled, screaming in pain. The other man, without being told, tossed his gun away and held up his hands.

"Who are you men working for?" Luke asked strongly. Again, he nervously looked at the plume of smoke, growing ever closer.

"None of your business, Mister!" exclaimed the man on the ground. "We've been well paid and we'll not betray them!"

"Get your tools and get that track repaired!" Luke ordered. His opponents glanced at each other.

"We'll not!" said the wounded man, rising to his feet. He hopped on his good leg. "Nor can you make us!"

Luke leaned back in his saddle. He really didn't need this kind of delay or trouble. Still, he was stuck with it. He cocked back the hammer once more. "The way I see it, boys, we have two choices. You can either repair the track, or I'll have to shoot you and then flag down the train. I don't have time to do both." He looked at them coldly, and smiled. Again, he felt a calm settle over him, and a buzzing fill his ears. He watched for any twitch, any movement that would make the decision.

The pair glanced at each other, then shrugged. They picked up the wrenches and began to slowly beat down the end of the rail that had been lifted.

"Make sure you bolt it proper, as well," Luke said, splitting attention between the men and the rapidly approaching train. It was moving at a fair clip, nearly forty miles an hour. He wasn't sure they would finish in time.

"Keep up the pace, gentlemen. I'm afraid I've not the temperament today for idleness." He tapped a heel against Star's flank and was pleased by her smooth move sideways so he had a better line of sight on the wounded man. The pair grumbled and muttered under their breath, but kept to their task.

The train was almost upon them when the last twist of the bolt secured the rail. "Now, gentlemen, we have an appointment with the Sheriff. Let's find your mounts." The men moved toward him, but at the last minute, jumped over the tracks, just as the train passed by. The engineer smiled and waved at Luke, not even noticing the gun in his hand. He blew the whistle at the bridge crossing and continued over the bridge without event. Luke watched the rail closely for any fault, but it held admirably. He was well aware that by the time the train passed, the men would be long gone. He'd simply have to inform the Sheriff when he reached Glenwood. Perhaps they could mount a posse.

# CHAPTER 31

Maribelle sat in the front room doing needlepoint. The cloth was so close to her face, she had to move back with each draw of the needle so she didn't poke herself in the nose.

She glanced up when her mother entered the back door. Her arms were laden with potatoes from the garden. She'd offered to help earlier, but her mother insisted she complete her needlework.

"Afternoon, Miss Maribelle."

Her heart stopped. She looked up in panic. Colonel Ballister stood in front of her, looking supremely nervous. She tried to give the appearance of nonchalance, but knew she failed.

"I've nothing to say to you, Colonel," she said frostily. Her hands betrayed her. She was trembling so much she could barely hold her needle. She set aside the sampler and placed her hands in her lap. She didn't meet his gaze.

"I know I've done nothing to make you want to speak to me, Maribelle," he said softly, turning his hat in his hands, "but I hope you'll believe me when I say it was pure fear and foolishness that caused my actions."

He stepped forward and she looked up, to her chagrin. He reached into his coat pocket and held out a small wooden box. She noticed that his hand trembled too. She took the oblong box with the tiny gold clasp, and he backed up a step. He returned to spinning his hat as she opened the box. It was filled with thin tissue paper, and more paper wrapped around a lightweight object inside.

Luke cleared his voice and spoke. There was a nervous edge to it. "Your father and I decided it wouldn't be proper to ask you to set up housekeeping unless you could see to do it." He moved from foot to foot, but stopped when he realized what he was doing, forcing himself to stand firmly.

"However, if you were to say 'no,'" he concluded, "then please consider this an apology for my earlier rudeness."

Maribelle had just finished unwrapping the object in the box. Thick pieces of glass were set into a thin gold frame. The inside of the box bore the mark of the optical doctor she had visited a year or more ago. Of course, that was before Father took to his bed. After that, she had never again spoken of her sight. She opened the glasses, and looped them around her ears.

The world snapped into sharp focus. She looked at the room as though she had never seen it. The draperies she and her mother had made were beautiful — thick red cotton, all the way from Boston, with delicate lace underneath! She stood and walked around the room in awe.

Is this what people saw every day? The rug had a colorful pattern she had never noticed, and the chair was a perfect match. She ruffled the delicate fringe on a lampshade with a grin. She looked over at Luke, embarrassed at her preoccupation with the decorations. Her breathing stilled as she saw him fully for the first time. Lord, he was even more handsome than she'd thought. Speechless, she stared at him for a long moment before she realized what he had said.

"Set up housekeeping?" she asked haltingly. She felt dizzy and lightheaded.

Luke nodded. "If you've a mind. Your father has already granted his approval."

Maribelle could think of no words to say! She squealed girlishly and threw herself forward. She wrapped her arms around Luke's waist and tightened her grip around his ribs until he gasped in pain. She never noticed. He stood with his arms out, unsure what to do. Eventually, Luke returned the hug and held her close. He smiled warmly. For an answer, it would do.

He couldn't imagine any celebration in Aspen that could be so fine as the quiet gaiety he'd found in the small Glenwood Springs home.

# CHAPTER 32

John McMurtrie sat on top of one of the boxcars, watching the celebration. Lord, but he was glad this job was over!

Powder blasts echoed through the cañon and colored rockets streaked from the mine entrances as the Special finally arrived — nearly two hours late! It was an event to be remembered. Whoops, laughter, and gunshots filled the air as the genteel of Denver mingled with the deliriously happy, hard-rock miners of Aspen. It was quite a party! The miners certainly took their rejoicing more seriously than the more sedate citizens of Glenwood!

John took a swig from a bottle he had liberated from one of the local taverns, after filling his belly with the fine barbeque served by the residents. He looked down as a couple of his men stumbled around on the ground below him. Their clumsy movements contradicted a serious discussion about whether to head to the next job, or take a day to rest. McMurtrie smiled. Ah, the sweet fever — there was nothing like it!

The air smelled like snow, and John took a deep breath of it from high on his perch. He'd found this position so that he could both watch the party, and revel in the marvel of the track and yard surrounding him. Word from Colonel Ricker was that the Midland had not yet completed their track to Frying Pan. The news had caused cheers on the train. All of the visitors from Denver were buoyant about reaching the mountain retreat, and vowed to return. Moffat had briefly looked for Luke, but quickly forgot him when the photographer arrived. John glanced toward the hotel where O'Malley slept, oblivious to the turmoil around him. He had gold enough to bring his wife here. John suspected Luke would soon have a wife, as well. In a few weeks, John could return to his own family.

He didn't care about the tourism, nor the freight. The track had reached Aspen, and General Palmer's dream was fulfilled. Soon, under Moffat's leadership, John knew the Rio Grande would reach the coal beds of New Castle and then Grand Junction. He hoped he would live long enough to see the Colorado line connect to Palmer's Denver & Rio Grande Western line in Utah, and then to the shores of California.

McMurtrie smiled broadly. Yes, it had been hard, but they had done it! The Rio Grande had won! He had dutifully attended the parade and ceremonies, where the mayor of Aspen had given a long-winded speech that celebrated the arrival of the "iron horse" to Aspen. Yet John thought he preferred the quickly written words by a local poet. He raised his bottle in a salute to all of the proud men who had made their mark on this land, and quietly recited the rhyme again:

> Then here's to our Aspen, her youth and her age,
> We welcome the railroad, say farewell to the stage;
> And whatever our lot and wherever we be,
> Here's God Bless forever the D. and R. G![6]

# ENDNOTES

[1]The 'Grand Cañon of the Grand' was renamed 'Glenwood Canyon' shortly after the arrival of the railroad in Glenwood Springs in 1887. The Colorado River was known as the Grand River prior to a bill signed in the 1902 Colorado legislature.

[2]The October 8, 1887 edition of *The Ute Chief* reported that "The contract for grading the Denver and Rio Grande extension from Red Cliff to Glenwood Springs had been let to Messrs. Carlisle, Price & McGarock, the well known railroad contractors, for the sum of $2,000,000, and it was stipulated in the contract that the grade should be completed and ready for the reception of cross ties and iron by the 1st of October."

[3]Now known as Basalt.

[4]The Glenwood Springs Western Union Telegraph office was known as the "uptown office," and the Rio Grande station as the "downtown office."

[5]On the day the Special train carrying David Moffat and his passengers was to arrive, a switch train engineer accidentally blew three blasts on his whistle, causing the celebration to begin in Aspen too early — by an hour and a half!

[6]Robert F. Bartlett, "Aspen: The Mining Community, 1870-1893," *Aspen Daily Times*, November 2, 1887. Denver Westerners Brand Book, 1950.

# BIBLIOGRAPHY/
# SUGGESTED READING

**BOOKS:**

Athearn, Dr. Robert, *"The Denver and Rio Grande Western Railroad"* (previously published under title: *"Rebel of the Rockies"*), Bison Press, 1977.

Haley, John L., *"Wooing a Harsh Mistress: Glenwood Canyon's Highway Odyssey,"* Canyon Communications, 1994.

**ARTICLES:**

*"Denver and Rio Grande, The,"* Fortune, 40 (1949), 97-105, 210-16.

*"History of the Denver and Rio Grande Railway,"* and *"Construction of the Denver & Rio Grande,"* Kansas State Historical Society, Santa Fe Railway Archives, RR928.22.

*"Irish Sports — Hurling,"* Gaelic Athletic Association, original rules http://www.gaa.ie/sports/hurling/oldrules.html.

*The Ute Chief* (predecessor to *The Glenwood Post*), April, 1887, through November, 1887.

Bradley, Glenn D., *"Builders of the Santa Fe,"* The Santa Fe Magazine, Volume VIII, Number 11, October 1914.

Bryant, Keith L., *"History of the Atchison, Topeka and Santa Fe Railway,"* University of Nebraska Press, 1974.

Ellis, Erl H., *"A Broad Gauge Tail on a Narrow Gauge Dog,"* Westerners Brand Book, 1954 (Denver, 1955), pp. 157-73 (used for general engineering details).

Jackson, William S., *"Record vs. Reminiscence, The,"* Westerners Brand Book, 1946 (Denver, 1947).

Le Massena, Robert A., *"The Royal Gorge,"* The Denver Westerners Monthly Roundup, Vol. XXI, Number 11, November 1965.

Lipsey, John J., "*J.J. Hagerman, Building of the Colorado Midland,*" Westerners Brand Book, 1954 (Denver, 1955), pp. 113-114.

Shoemaker, Len, "*Early Days in Garfield County,*" Westerners Brand Book, 1947 (Denver, 1948), pp. 309-331.

Sumberg, Jeff, "*The Hoosac Tunnel, on the Boston & Maine RR,*" http://www.intac.com/~jsumberg/hoosac.html.

Thode, Jackson C., LM, "*To Aspen and Beyond,*" Westerners Brand Book, 1964 (Denver, 1965), pp. 175-223.
*(Authors' Note: This article was our primary source for the day-to-day happenings of the construction. It deciphers and organizes the poorly written, sometimes caustic, telegrams between the construction crew and the Denver management. Many of the telegrams written into this novel are verbatim. We highly recommend this article to those who would like to read more about the construction.)*

Warman, Cy, "*The Grand Canyon War,*" Santa Fe Magazine, January, 1923.

**MISCELLANEOUS DOCUMENTS:**
Archived records of the Denver & Rio Grande Railway and Denver & Rio Grande Railroad (successor after bankruptcy), Colorado Railroad Museum, Golden, Colorado.

Archived records of the Denver & Rio Grande Railroad, Collection 513, Colorado Historical Society, Denver, Colorado.

Original telegrams to and from the Glenwood Canyon construction crew from officers and managers of the D&RG, Colorado Railroad Museum, Golden, Colorado.

Construction engineering documents, Santa Fe Railway Project for the Kansas State Historical Society, successor to Denver & Rio Grande Railroad.

Construction engineering documents and blueprints, The Burlington Northern and Santa Fe Railway Company, successor to Santa Fe Railway Co. (each company had different documents).